AN AVALON ROMANCE

READY, WILLING
AND . . . ABEL
Linda Lattimer

Lynne Murphy, a children's book illustrator, moves to the mountains of Tennessee for some quiet solitude away from everyone and to look for some inspiration. She finds more than she ever expected when her next door neighbor saves her from a near catastrophe on a ladder.

Abel Mason has taken refuge from the world for a lot longer than Lynne has. His wife died three years ago and since then, he has shut himself off from everyone—even his family—alone in his cabin with his trusty dog, Samson.

But soon, as they spend time together, Lynne opens his eyes to the world—coloring his life with hope and joy once again. Can Abel let go of the past and grab hold of the future standing right in front of him? Or will he let fears from the past consume him? Lynne has a difficult road ahead, but it is one that she is ready and willing to traverse.

READY, WILLING AND ... ABEL

•

Linda Lattimer

AVALON BOOKS
NEW YORK

Published by Thomas Bouregy & Co., Inc.
160 Madison Avenue, New York, NY 10016

PRINTED IN THE UNITED STATES OF AMERICA
ON ACID-FREE PAPER
BY HADDON CRAFTSMEN, BLOOMSBURG, PENNSYLVANIA

For Bob . . . there aren't enough words to express how I feel . . .
but you always supported me and told me I could do anything
I set my mind to . . . and I thank you always for that. For the
good times and even the bad . . . thank you for everything.
This first one is for you.

Acknowledgments

My thanks always to our Heavenly Father above who watches over us.

My gratitude and appreciation to Mira S. Park who believed in me and gave me the opportunity to be a part of the Avalon family.

My thanks always to my dear friend, Carolyn Brown, who told me to never give up. To Cheri Jetton, another good friend who was there for me too. As well as Roni Denholtz, Ludima Gus Burton, Shelley Galloway and Nancy J. Parra. And to Gloria, all of you were there for me when there was so much heartache in my life. Your prayers, cards, and love were well received when Bob was in the hospital. Thanks for all your support in everything.

To my wonderful daughters who have supported me always no matter what. Marvetta, Suzanne, and Lisa Renee, I love you. And my son-in-laws, TR, Richard and Tommy, the greatest sons any mom could ask for. And four wonderful grandsons, Allen, Robert, Dylan and Dakota.

For my parents. Daddy, you are no longer here, but you did love my writing.

For Cindy, Mikey, Tommy, Zachary, Mike and Stella, for your support in all my efforts, thanks for all your love, encouragement, and kind words.

For Sarah White and all my School Nutrition friends and co-workers in Nashville; thanks for supporting me.

And for Joe: Thanks for going to the library for me and bringing home all those great Avalon books to read.

Chapter One

Lynne hauled the last box out of the truck and carried it into the cabin. It was something that she had looked forward to for a very long time. After making a couple of sales with her drawings for the children's books, she had managed to make enough to pay off her truck and purchase the small two-bedroom loft cabin outside of Gatlinburg, Tennessee. It was a distance from New York City but she had assured Mack that with her laptop and drawings, she would be able to get them to him pronto. She would still meet all deadlines.

Sure, he had argued with her when she had purchased the truck, declaring that a petite woman had no business driving an extended cab truck, but it was something that she had always desired. It was good to make deliveries. To sleep out under the stars when she went on her camping trips. And it certainly came in handy when she made the big move. She had shown him that she had no problem in handling the vehicle.

1

She placed the box upstairs in the bedroom then looked out the window. The month of October had been the perfect time to move. The leaves were changing beautifully here. The bears would all be hibernating until the spring and summer months. She had seen them out many times when she visited during the end of April. This time she would have to really make sure the garbage cans were carefully locked down.

She crossed her arms and whirled around the room, then glided down the stairs. For two years she had waited patiently for the owners to decide if they really wanted to sell the cabin. She had crossed fingers and toes waiting for them to make the decision. When Jed Mason phoned her with the good news, she jumped at the offer. The price had been perfect. The owners were even installing a satellite dish for her since the reception wasn't that great in the hideaway.

Lynne inhaled a breath of fresh air as she walked out on the front porch. This indeed was what she truly wanted. Peace, solitude, and beauty. She spotted a squirrel scampering across a tree branch. "I can't believe this is really mine. Well, not quite. I paid off the truck, but on the cabin I still owe half. But a few more drawings and bingo, I can probably say it's all mine. Hard work and socking away savings can in time give a person what they really want."

She noticed the squirrel standing, gazing her way.

"I know what you're thinking. I'm not getting any younger and I should have someone to share this place with. Well, that someone hasn't come along yet." She gave the squirrel a lopsided grin. "I almost had someone, but I discovered that he just wasn't what the future had in store for me, Mr. Squirrel."

The squirrel gave her a guarded stare then scampered off.

"Guess he didn't like my company. Had to have been a male."

She walked down the pathway a bit and admired the luxury of the colorful leaves. The trees were so plentiful. When the snowfall arrived, she would most likely be trapped up this way for three or four days. Firewood would have to be chopped. She noticed that the Parkinsons had left her a full bin. They were such nice people. She'd liked them since the first time that she had rented the cabin from them.

She stood outside gazing at the lovely log cabin. There was a loft with a queen-size bed upstairs with an adjoining bathroom. Downstairs was a living room and kitchen combined, separated by an island and bar counter for sharing meals. A dining table off to the side near the back door, which led to a long back porch with swing and outdoor grill. There was a small basement that housed the washer and dryer but it was roomy enough to even add a pool table later if she wished.

There was another smaller bedroom downstairs with a bathroom that housed a huge whirlpool. She could hardly wait to feel the stirring sensation of the water soothing her tired, worn muscles.

The fireplace in the living room was spacious and really put warmth throughout the whole cabin. She might even decide to start a fire tonight. The temperature did drop considerably in the mountain area. She walked by the truck to lock the doors.

She wanted to take one more quick glimpse around before she went inside to finish unpacking and putting everything in its proper place. Her eyes met with the corner of the roof near the satellite dish and noticed that the dish was leaning over slightly. She was glad that she had decided to buy that ladder. She needed to take care of this little matter now.

Abel threw the ball a couple more times at his yellow Labrador retriever. The dog easily found the ball and returned it to his owner. It was something that he looked forward to whenever his owner was able to take time out to play.

"Good boy," Abel offered as he scratched Samson's head. "Sorry I haven't had much time to spend with you lately. Been busy with my work. Tell you what—why don't I throw the ball once more before I go back inside and check the stew? Got some simmering in the slow cooker. Are you ready? Here goes."

Abel threw the ball farther this time as Samson chased after it. This time Samson didn't return. Instead he stood wagging his tail and barking at something below.

"What is it, Samson?" Abel said, taking strides to reach him. "Don't tell me you've seen another squirrel. All you do is bark at them. Never once have you gone after one."

His eyes followed where Samson was barking. He noticed the black Dodge truck near the cabin below his. His pathway led to the cabin that the Parkinsons owned but he hadn't seen them in a good while. The last he heard they were trying to sell the place.

"It's all right boy. I think the cabin has new owners. Come on, let's go." He patted the dog's head.

But Samson wouldn't budge. He barked twice then pulled at Abel's sleeve.

"Samson, it's okay, boy. They're just new neighbors."

Once more Samson pulled at Abel's sleeve.

"All right, we'll go meet them," he said as he started down the hill. But no sooner had he gotten a few steps that he observed the reason for Samson's harsh barking. "What is that girl doing?" His feet raced faster down the hill.

Lynne put the last screw in the board and started to situate her footing back on the ladder when it started to slip in the dirt. A sudden stir of panic seized her. There was no way she was going to level it. In moments she and the ladder would be crashing to the ground and there would be no one in miles to hear her when she screamed for help.

Stupid silly woman, what were you thinking of? If I could only get the ladder to swing to the left then maybe I could fall on the upper side. If I allow it to fall to the right, I'll roll down the hill. Me and my macho image, she scolded herself.

She inhaled a breath and with all her might started to move the ladder to swing to the left. But her attempt only caused it to shift backwards. A loud scream issued from her lips as she went barreling down backwards, arms and legs swinging from the ladder.

It all happened so fast. All Lynne could concentrate on was where she was going to land. On rocks, on grass, in a tree? And would the fall break a limb or her back? She'd just invested in this cabin and bingo, now she would be out of commission. Why hadn't she waited for Jed to come up and help? She closed her eyes and said a prayer.

She made a thump as she landed safely into arms. She was shaking and her eyes were still closed as she prayed for safety. There was the sound of a dog barking.

"Miss," Abel said as his breathing slowly returned to normal. "You can open your eyes now. I made it just in time." He noticed that she was trembling and with good reason.

Slowly Lynne opened her eyes. Was she dreaming? Had she hit her head and an angel from heaven saved her? If this was an angel he had the clearest blue eyes that she had ever seen. Mesmerizing. It was as if she were in a hypnotic trance. Her arms wound up around his neck. She couldn't remember how, they just did.

"Miss, you're shaking like a leaf. You're going to be okay. I'm glad my dog noticed something. I thought I wouldn't make it in time. You took a chance climbing up on that ladder that way. You should have allowed your husband to do that. No woman needs to be climbing up on a ladder with no one around."

Well, ol' Mr. Blue Eyes might be captivating, but he sure didn't have to scold her for climbing a ladder.

She inhaled a breath. "You can put me down now. I think I'll be fine."

"Just what were you doing up there anyway?"

"I noticed the dish was loose. I wanted to adjust it."

"And that couldn't have waited?"

She didn't need a lecture from a perfect stranger.

"Sir, you can stand me on my feet now. I wasn't aware my falling in your arms was going to earn me so much scolding."

Abel planted her on her feet, making sure that she was fully grounded and able to stand. She had been light as a feather in his arms. Just a petite girl. He was a little over five-feet-nine but she was still short. Was she even five-two? She was wearing a pair of white short overalls with a blue knit top.

"I didn't mean to scold. When I saw you hanging on that ladder my heart stopped. Then when you went tumbling down—" He exhaled a breath as he walked over to the ladder. "Come here."

She followed.

"If that ladder had gone the other way, you see that backdrop? You could have severely hurt yourself. Where's your husband? Couldn't you have waited for him to take care of that? Or the Parkinsons? Of course, I haven't seen them in a while. What, was there a pressing soap opera you needed to watch?"

Her brown eyes shot into his blue ones. He had a full mass of light brown hair that had been ruffled by the fast run that he had made down the hill. He had a wisp of hair lapping over his eyes a little. And for a moment she considered moving it but decided against it.

"The Parkinsons installed the satellite dish for me but I guess something triggered it to come loose on one of the bolts. They no longer live here. I bought the cabin from them. I wasn't getting ready to watch any soaps. And I don't have a husband to fix things for me." Her eyes expanded at her last remark. What was wrong with her? Rule number one: never offer any information like that to a complete stranger, especially out here in the woods away from civilization.

He noticed how she suddenly froze. "No husband?"

Her eyes shot to the front of the cabin. Could she make it in time to get to a phone? To lock the cabin so he couldn't get inside?

"You don't have to be startled, miss." He extended his hand. "Hi, I'm Abel. I heard through the grapevine that the Parkinsons were considering selling the place. Seems they even mentioned to me that Jed had it on the market for them. I had no idea they had already sealed the deal. This here is Samson."

She pumped her hand in Abel's. "Didn't mean to cause a panic there. I'd forgotten one rule of thumb— don't ever offer you don't have a husband, I've been told."

"True, but if you went around doing that all the time, you might not get asked out on dates." He smiled and Lynne noticed white teeth all straight and perfect.

She knelt down and rubbed the top of Samson's head. "So I owe you for sending your owner my way. Good to meet you, Samson."

Samson barked.

Lynne stood to her feet again.

"He likes you."

"What?"

"Samson. He hasn't cottoned to any woman coming near him for three years. You're the first after all this time."

"Oh really. Who was the first?" Lynne asked with a smile.

Abel looked at his watch. "Oh, I just remembered, I've got some stew simmering in the slow cooker. I better go check it," he said, disregarding her question. He lifted the ladder. "I'll sit this around near the other side of the front porch, but you have to promise me that you won't climb it unless someone is around to supervise or hold it."

"I assure you that I will not be that gullible again. I appreciate you coming to my rescue, Abel."

"No problem." He pointed up the hill. "Samson and I only live right atop there. There's a pathway that swings down this way or you can take the road that swings around. Come on, Samson. I'll race you home. We need to check on our supper."

Lynne watched as he and Samson made steps to the pathway. She shook her head. She hadn't even bothered introducing herself to him. She wondered if she would even see him anymore. He was a rather handsome man with a slightly tanned face. What had he been wearing? Oh yes, brown boots, blue jeans, and a red plaid flannel shirt. Reminded her of a logger. And the way his arms had caught her and held her . . .

But those blue eyes. She could admire those eyes all day if she had to. And that hair. Why had she wanted to touch that one strand that seemed to feather across his forehead? A grin pasted her lips. Scolding, lecturing. She probably would have done the same thing. He was only warning her to be careful. He had avoided her question, though, about whom Samson had been fond of before her.

"Abel, huh?" she said as he headed toward the door of the cabin. "What was that saying—ready, willing, and Abel? You silly girl. It's ready, willing, and able." Yeah, but this Abel she liked much better. She would have to ask Jed about him on her next trip into town.

Samson drank some water from his bowl then flopped on the front porch while Abel went inside to check the stew.

So a single woman purchased the cabin. Quite pretty too in those overalls. Brown eyes, small nose, nice lips, and shoulder-length auburn hair. She had been like a feather in his arms. But she had no business being up on that roof with no one around. Her perfume was still tickling his nostrils. Sort of like jasmine. Why was he even thinking about her? He had promised himself never to look at another woman again.

Again his thoughts stirred back to her. She'd just moved in. Perhaps she hadn't had time to prepare a meal with all that packing and stuff. No husband and driving a truck? How did she even handle that? And Samson liked her. That dog had gone to no woman since . . . Well, he had gone to Mrs. Parkinson, but that was different. She was fifty years old. She had sort of been like a grandmother to him. And Samson always visited her practically every day. This girl Samson liked. Perhaps that was a sign to start over.

Abel walked back outside to the porch. He poured some dog food into Samson's dish then went inside to stir the stew again. He gave it a couple of swirls with the wooden spoon as his mind continued thinking. No. There would be no starting over. He was finished with women and his family. The hurt was still there. After three long years, though, this woman was stirring thoughts in his head that had been closed. He walked out to the porch and sat in the rocker. Samson looked up at him, his tail lightly slapping against some of the firewood on the porch. He barked twice.

Abel cast an eye his way. What was it about that dog today? He actually liked the petite woman. He had liked Ilene as well.

Samson released another bark. Abel leaned over in the rocker and gave Samson a couple of pats on the head. Abel shook his head. He wasn't sure about this. Ilene had been very special. Deep in his heart he had always felt that once you lost a special person, it was hard to find another one.

Samson made a grunting noise.

Abel leaned his head against the back of the rocker and thought for a moment. Maybe he should take her some stew. New and all and just settling in. Yeah, she probably had been busy unpacking. No time to prepare anything.

Samson yelped another bark, this one louder.

Abel shifted in the rocker. He released a sigh. He had told himself that he wouldn't get close to anyone ever again. Ilene was so unique. A beautiful woman who would always stay in his heart. So what was this sensation pulling at his heartstrings? Why couldn't he rub this feeling out of his heart? Just erase it like an eraser rubbing chalk off a chalkboard.

Samson sat up and moved by the rocker, making a whimpering noise. Abel looked into Samson's brown eyes. Strange, the color of Samson's eyes was the same as the young woman's. He released a smile. His best friend wouldn't steer him wrong about anything. If Samson liked the young woman then Abel would go pay her a visit. What would it really hurt? But that would be as far as it went.

Samson wagged his tail and let out a low howl.

"Yes, let's take her some stew. I wonder does she know she never gave me her name."

*   *   *

Lynne was slipping on a pair of jeans and a light-weight yellow pullover sweater when she happened to see the squirrel outside her bathroom window. He sat perched near the roof and appeared to be holding a nut of some sort in his hands.

She watched as the squirrel played with the nut. Her mind slowly drifted to the handsome man who had caught her in his very strong arms. He did appear to be a nice sort of man. And the dog, Samson, his coat was beautiful. He had taken right up with her as if he had known her always. She thought of preparing Abel something since he was so kind to save her life. She crossed her arms, hugging her chest. If she had taken a tumble she would have been most miserable.

She inhaled a breath. Taking the brush, she gave her hair a good brushing then pulled it back, snapping it with a barrette. Time to unpack some more boxes, then maybe take a nice evening stroll before it got too late. She still couldn't believe that she had a cabin to call her home.

Her foot was about to take the last step down from the bedroom when there was a knock at the front door. Peeping through the edge of the curtain, she got a glimpse of Abel.

"Hello again," she said, opening the door.

He eyed her from head to toe. She had been pretty in the short overall outfit but now she was breathtaking, refreshed.

"Samson and I thought that we would share the stew with you. Unpacking and all, you probably haven't had time to cook. By the look of things, you appear to be going out."

"Oh no. I felt kind of grubby being up on that ladder

so I changed clothes. Thought I might go for a stroll before night settled in. The stew smells delicious. Please come in."

She noticed that Samson curled up near the edge of the porch.

"Oh, Samson prefers the outdoors. When it gets knee-deep in snow he'll come in and sit by the fire. But I had to make his own little doghouse for him."

"He seems right at home."

"He used to visit Mrs. Parkinson."

Lynne shut the door. "Here, you can sit the basket on the counter. I've got a glass heat plate to sit the pan on. We could even sit here. That is if you don't mind a bar stool."

"No. Fine with me." He sat the basket down then pulled the pot out and placed it on the glass holder. "I didn't know if you had unpacked any dishes so I brought some bowls and spoons."

"You've thought of everything—ice tea, glasses, French bread, even napkins. I like this basket. Did you buy it at one of the craft shops in Gatlinburg?"

"No, Il . . ." He stopped. "It's one that's been in the family for a long time. A family member made it."

Lynne shook her head and admired the beauty of it. "I wish that I could make something like that. You should suggest your family member sell these. I would be willing to buy one."

He set the bowls, napkins, and spoons on the counter but never mentioned anymore about the basket. Lynne noticed he suddenly turned quiet and didn't refer to the basket again.

Abel dipped out the stew then placed some of the sliced French bread on the napkins.

"I don't know why I call this stew. It has hardly any meat inside. I have more vegetables than anything else swimming in it. I need to go into town and buy a few groceries. I always wait until the last minute."

"I guess living alone one doesn't think much of keeping the kitchen stocked. At least I find myself forgetting," she said while spooning a bite of the hot stew in her mouth. "This is really good, Abel. I'm not much of a meat eater myself. You will have to give me your recipe. I am tasting different flavors of spices." She took a napkin and blotted her mouth. "Oh, I almost forgot again. Seems when I introduced myself by falling into your arms, I failed to give you my name. Lynne Murphy."

He took a bite of the bread and watched how she delicately ate. Lynne Murphy. The name Lynne was pretty, just as she was. This was so strange and new to him. Why after three years did he feel compelled to spend time with this young woman? There was something about her that was drawing him like a magnet to her. He would never forget how she felt when she landed in his arms.

"I thought about that later. I'm sure being a single woman and all you are cautious about tossing out your name to people, especially men."

"Yes. I failed miserably when you inquired about my husband."

"I just caught you off guard."

She lifted the glass of tea to her lips then smiled after she swallowed almost half of it. Not only could this man cook, he could make delicious tea. "Abel, I'm just glad you came along and caught me. I could see me laid up in traction or my leg in cement. Again let me express to you how good this is. Even the tea. Do you mind if I have another glass full and a bowl of the stew?"

He filled her glass then placed some more of the steaming stew in the bowl.

"I normally don't eat seconds, but this—okay, I've already mentioned how good it is."

He handed her another slice of bread and grinned.

"All right. One more. I'll walk it off later."

"I don't think you need to worry about walking anything off."

She sent him a warm smile. Franklin had never said anything like that to her.

Lynne washed up the few dishes while Abel checked on Samson. Since he had eaten before they arrived, Abel handed him a bone. He usually carried one in his pocket wrapped for when they took their strolls.

After drying the pan, she placed it inside the basket with the other dried and cleaned dishes. She couldn't get over the lovely oval-shaped basket. Twice he hadn't wished to speak of someone. She wondered why but wouldn't dare pry. He seemed like a very nice neighbor and she wanted to keep him as her friend. With winter soon to arrive and the snow, she wanted to have close neighbors in case she got stranded.

"Did Samson eat his bone?"

"Yes, every bite. I would have helped with the dishes." He stood at the door with his back leaning against it and his ankles crossed.

"Absolutely not. You cooked the meal and brought it to me. I appreciate it, Abel."

"I guess that I should be going."

Do you have too? she wanted to ask. She liked him. He was easy to talk to.

"I guess that I should do some more unpacking."

He noticed the children's book displayed on the coffee table. She said no husband. Did she have kids? Surely not.

"You like children's books?" He picked it up and thumbed through it, then started to place it back on the table when he saw her name on the front of it. *Illustrated by Lynne Murphy.* His eyes turned to her. He opened the book back up and looked inside. "You did these?"

She walked over toward him. "Yes. That is what I do for a living."

"These are excellent. Do you only do illustrations for children's books?"

"I've done some other drawings that people have commissioned from me. I usually stick to children's books. It was something that I always wanted to do. Not only are the children intrigued by the story but also they love the pictures. I like to do a lot of drawings of children's books and take them to orphanages or the section of the hospital where all the sick children are housed. It really puts a smile on their sad faces."

"You are certainly good at what you do."

"Thank you."

"Well, I should be on my way. You mentioned a stroll, so I won't keep you any longer."

Abel, you can keep me for eternity. Why don't we go for a stroll together? What was wrong with her? Her thoughts had never been that forward with any man.

"Again, thank you for that splendid meal." Is that all she could think of repeating, was the meal?

"Consider it like a housewarming meal." He smiled from ear to ear.

"I will indeed."

Lynne patted Samson before they left. For a few minutes she stood out on the front porch and watched as they walked up the pathway. There would be no more unpacking tonight, nor any stroll. As she observed Abel and Samson step out of sight, she knew what she would give Abel for catching her from that fall.

Chapter Two

Jed Mason was busy going over some paperwork when Lynne tapped at his door then entered.

"Am I interrupting?"

"Never. Come in, Lynne. I was hoping that I would run into you." He rose from his chair and stepped to the other side of the desk. He gave her a warm hug. "I hope that everything is coming along with the cabin." He motioned for her to sit in the chair by his desk. He swung back around to his seat.

"Yes. Can't you seem me beaming?"

"Yes I can. I really think that you are my most happy customer."

"That I am. Sorry it's taken me this long to drop by. Been trying to get organized."

"Gwen and the boys were wondering when you would grace us with your presence again. Of course we both knew you wanted to settle in first. She did urge me to invite you over for dinner when I saw you."

"I couldn't impose with her expecting and all. In no time she will be having the baby."

"Doctor says the baby might arrive before Thanksgiving. That would be nice for all of us."

"It certainly would be. I would like to see the boys again too."

"They are always asking about their Aunt Lynne."

"Hardly. But I'm glad that they adopted me. You're the only real family I've had here since I've been coming to rent the cabin, with the exception of the Parkinsons."

"It has been our pleasure knowing you. So you're settling in with all the unpacking?"

"Oh yeah." A bubbly smile folded over her lips.

"You're pretty happy today."

"You didn't tell me that I had a very close neighbor. Kind of handsome too."

"Oh."

"Yes. In all the times that I have rented that cabin this is the first that I've seen him."

Jed rested his hands on his desk. "So you've already had a guest to come to your cabin?"

"I was doing a stupid thing. The satellite dish was lose so I climbed on a ladder."

"Lynne, that could have been dangerous."

"I quickly found out. Luckily a neighbor with his dog happened by and saved me from the fall. Guess you could say that I fell right into his arms. His dog, Samson, spotted me and lured him to my direction."

Jed arched his brows. "Samson?"

"Yes. A lovely golden Lab retriever. In fact he took

right up with me. Abel, the man who caught me, said he hadn't done that in a long time. He was all set to tell me the last person that Samson went to and he froze. He never mentioned any more on the subject. He even brought some stew that he had made to share with me that night. He seems really nice. Even mentioned your name."

He twirled his thumbs as he folded his hands on the desk. "Really?"

"Yes. After he introduced himself he mentioned how the Parkinsons said Jed had put the cabin on the market for them. You're the only Jed I know in these parts."

"Did he say anything else?"

"He had this lovely basket when he brought the food down to me. I inquired about it but again he froze. Said a family member made it. Jed, the basket was adorable."

"Yes, I know."

This time she raised a brow of concern.

"I want you to stay away from him, Lynne."

"Why?"

"He's trouble."

"He didn't appear to be any trouble."

"Appearances can be deceiving. Take my word—stay clear of him. You're too nice to get your heart broken."

"I don't understand, Jed. I mean, is he a convicted criminal or something? You're scaring me."

Jed exhaled a breath. "Lynne, he hasn't been around people in a long time. He's a hermit. He's been that way for three long years. I don't like the idea of him coming out to see you now. He only comes into town

when he needs something or when someone has some
work for him."

"What's wrong with that? Some people like privacy.
Why do you think I moved from New York to the
mountains here?"

"Anyone who doesn't want to be around family or
even give them the time of day should just be disre-
garded."

Lynne chewed on her bottom lip. There was something going on here. And now that she was really staring at Jed, and remembering Abel, her brain started
turning.

"What's Abel last name?"

"What?"

"If you know him so well, surely you know his last
name. He only introduced himself as Abel."

Jed leaned back in the huge black chair, swiveled
it, then came to a stop. "Abel Mason. He's my brother.
I guess that you could say he's the black sheep of the
family."

"I can see a resemblance now. So that makes him
off limits?"

"Lynne, there is a dark past to Abel. I don't want
you to get hurt. For the past three years he has done
nothing but shut me and my family out of his life."

"Perhaps he had good reason." She looked around
the office. "Look Jed, the man I met seems caring.
Correction—*was* caring. He acted as if he was troubled by something but he seems like he cares for
people. I don't know why the two of you can't get
along, but I like him. He's a lot nicer than the man I
left back in New York. That man had a double side
to him."

"You haven't known Abel as long as I have." He rubbed his forehead. "Just forget what I've said. Maybe he is changing. I would like to think so. Gwen has tried calling him since the incident but he doesn't want to talk to anyone. And the boys ask about their Uncle Abel. They miss him."

"Incident?"

"I shouldn't be saying anything."

"You opened the door."

"His wife died three years ago. He hasn't been the same since her death. He shut all of us out. Said we didn't understand what it was like to lose someone. Then right after the funeral he insisted that none of us had accepted her because she had Cherokee in her. We all loved Ilene. As for the basket, she made it. She was good with her hands. Her death barricaded him in that cabin for a long time."

"How did she die?"

"They were mountain climbing. Somehow she went too high and her foot slipped."

"He scolded me for climbing on that ladder."

"For good reason. I would have too. If it means anything, I do hope you can reach him. We want him back with us. The holidays are coming. We haven't sat down to share a meal with him since all this happened. With Gwen expecting a new baby, she desperately wants him to be a part of the family again. I can't press him to come back to our fold. Not only that, we just found out this baby is a girl. We were going to wait until it was born but Gwen suddenly said do the test. I mean, here she is, ready to pop soon and wants to know now. We would like to share the news with Abel."

Lynne rose to her feet. A grin formed over her lips. "I have a feeling that things are about to change, Jed."

"I hope you're right. I still want you to be careful. He still could be a time bomb about to explode."

She shook her head. "Not the man whose arms I landed in. This man was gentle."

Lynne placed another item in the shopping cart then turned to the other aisle when she bumped into Abel.

"So sorry, I didn't see . . ." A grin formed on her lips. "Abel. I see you're shopping too. You should have told me you were going to town—we could have ridden together."

He watched how the grin made her eyes sparkle. She was such a pretty woman. Today she was wearing her hair cascading down on her small shoulders. The blue jeans and yellow cotton shirt fit her as if she was a model on a magazine cover. What was it about her that was stirring his heartstrings? He had thought about her every night since he caught her in his arms. Remembering how his heart hammered when he saw her atop that ladder tumbling down, falling just like . . .

Lynne noticed how his face seemed to display different expressions. What was he thinking about?

"Abel?"

He scratched the top of his head. "I'm not in the habit of telling anyone where I'm going."

Was that spoken in a frosty way or was he just irritated to see her? She couldn't quite make it out. She thought of Jed's words.

"I didn't mean to intrude. I'll let you finish your

49974

shopping. Be sure to tell Samson I said hello." She grinned once more then turned the cart away.

A hand lightly touched her shoulder. "Lynne, I didn't mean for that to come out in a snappy way."

She rotated her head to see his hand resting on her shoulder. She recalled how it felt when she dropped into his arms. He removed his hand then turned her cart back around.

"I believe that you wanted to check the items in this aisle. There's enough room for the both of us." This time he grinned, then he smiled wide. "Tell you what, you could offer to give me a lift home. Samson and I walked."

"You walked?"

"It's only a three-mile hike if you take the pathway into town. Most of it is downhill."

"Yes, but that's *coming* downhill."

"So want to give us a lift?"

Her eyes searched his. The blue was incredible this morning. "I'll do better than that. You choose what you like to eat and I'll cook you a meal tonight. That is if I'm not intruding on your privacy."

"Got to feed Samson too."

"Oh, I will."

Lynne turned the steaks then tossed the salad. She watched as Abel poured some food in a dog bowl for Samson then placed it on the front porch.

"You didn't have to purchase him a dog bowl," Abel offered as he entered and started washing his hands.

"Yes I did. He might wander down this way hungry."

"And that's why you got the ten-pound bag of dog food?"

"Of course. You said he would visit Mrs. Parkinson."

"As long as he remembers where his home is."

"I don't think he would ever forget going home to you, Abel." *If I was Samson, I have a feeling that I wouldn't forget.*

Abel sniffed. "The steaks smell great. You didn't have to go to this trouble."

"I urged you to get what you wanted. Want to check on the potatoes? I think they're ready. Just need to get the butter and sour cream. The steaks are ready too. Grab a plate and let's eat."

Abel eased over toward the stove to check the potatoes. He slightly brushed against Lynne. He felt a warm current strike him. He wondered if she had felt it. Her perfume again tickled his nostrils. Still he wondered why he was feeling this way about another woman. No, it was only a payback dinner. He had to remember Ilene, her memory. They had loved each other more than anything. No one could take her place. All he had now was Samson. That was enough. He would have to make sure nothing ever happened to his dog. But he had felt something when he brushed by Lynne. Something that had sent a warm feeling soaring into his heart.

Lynne got the plates and put the steaks on them. Abel had brushed against her and she had felt a slight shock. Was it static of some sort? No. It was that warm surge again that speared all the way down to her toes making them want to curl like little Santa-elves' shoes. Jed didn't really know the man who was standing in her kitchen helping her to prepare a meal. This man was warm and fun to be with. She had only arrived in her new home and this man was sending wonderful currents of warmth all through her.

Together they shared a quiet dinner and afterward Abel helped with the dishes. When they were done he invited her for an evening stroll.

"I love the mountains," Lynne said as they paused atop a hill. "I wanted to go hiking in the Smoky Mountains before it turned too cold."

"We could always go one weekend before the snow arrives."

We. He had said *we.* "I think that I would enjoy that." Samson nudged against her leg. She knelt down and hugged his neck. "You enjoying this walk, boy?"

He wagged his tail then barked. A truck was slowly coming up their way. Lynne stood to her feet.

"Looks like Gene Warner is paying a visit."

"You know him, Abel?"

"Yeah."

The truck came to a halt but the engine continued to idle.

"Abel, just the man I was looking for." Gene turned his eyes to Lynne. "Miss." He tipped his hat.

"Gene, this is my new neighbor, Lynne Murphy. She bought the Parkinson place. Lynne, this is Gene Warner."

"Good to have you here, Miss Murphy. I believe you'll like this area."

"Already do. Is your place near?"

"Down near Gatlinburg. Got me a small craft store downtown. I didn't mean to interrupt your walk. I heard Abel had come into town today. Sorry I missed you, Abel. I wondered if you could work on another project for me? The last one you did . . . well, that couple took it back home to South Carolina with them. Now that some of the folks there saw your work they want to order one too. Already sent me a check for half to start the work and will pay you the rest when it's finished. I got part of the supplies in the back of my truck. Got the layout of how they want it too."

Abel leaned and looked at the supplies. The last time he made the gazebo and bench it took up most of his time. Of course it kept his mind busy too. He wouldn't have time to spend with Lynne. Why was he thinking that? He wasn't going to ever get involved with a woman again. Not after Ilene. No one could ever take her place. Yet there was something that was slowly drawing him to Lynne.

"Got quite a bit back here, Gene."

"Gonna have some more too. They want a swing to go with theirs."

"That's a lot of work."

"They're willing to pay extra."

"Take it on up to the house. I'll take Miss Murphy home then meet you there."

"If you need to ride on with Mr. Warner, I'll be okay, Abel," Lynne offered.

"No. I invited you for a stroll. I'll take you to your door."

So formal. Was he embarrassed with her now? She nodded.

"Miss Murphy, it was a pleasure to meet you."

"Same here, Mr. Warner."

Lynne watched the truck drive away then started walking back toward the cabin.

"Is that your line of work, Abel?" she asked as they approached the front of the cabin. "You labor in wood-work?"

"I do some."

"Your work must be good for people to commission it from a first-time show. I would like to see your handiwork. Perhaps I could walk up and see some of your crafts."

"No."

She noted how he didn't even hesitate in his answer.

"I prefer my privacy, Lynne. Nothing personal. I don't want visitors."

She rubbed the toe of her tennis shoe at the rocks near the step of the porch. "Well, thanks for the stroll."

"Thanks for the dinner. I enjoyed it. Samson, tell Lynne good night."

Samson raised his paw and Lynne shook it, then gave him a huge hug.

"You know, Abel, if you ever need a ride or you need to pick up supplies, well, I don't normally lend out my truck to anyone. What I'm saying is since we are neigh-bors if you need to use it let me know." She wanted to say *since you are Jed's brother* but she couldn't allow that to slip. He might suspect that she was out snooping about him.

"That's very kind, Lynne."

"Perhaps we could get together for another stroll or share another meal together. I wouldn't have to come up. I could call you and meet you halfway with the meal."

He rubbed his chin and looked around the area then focused his eyes with hers. "Lynne, when I'm busy working I want to be left alone. The two meals we shared, the stroll, they weren't dates. You're a new neighbor. I was trying to be hospitable. And I don't want you climbing on any more ladders."

Dates? Neighbor? Dates? Is that what he thought they were gearing toward? "You only say that 'cause you are thinking of—" She quickly bit her tongue.

A flash of concern appeared on his face.

"What I meant was my safety. Even Jed said . . ." *Uh-oh.*

"Jed Mason? You spoke to him?"

"Yes. You know I went through his office to get this cabin. You even said you heard he had it on the market. I saw him today. I wanted to tell him how I had settled into the cabin."

"Did you mention me to him?"

"I casually through conversation stated how you were my neighbor and had caught me. He said I had no business being on the ladder either."

Abel crossed his arms. "Go on."

"That was it. I expressed how this caring man happened by and I landed in his arms."

"And nothing was introduced to you about me?"

"Should there have been? I wasn't there but a few minutes to tell him how I was settling in. Again let me stress that he did help me get the cabin." She gave him a slight grin, hoping he would drop the matter. She didn't want any harsh feelings between them.

He lowered his hands to his side, then gave her a lopsided grin. "No. Since I stay to myself, I guess I'm just curious what others might think of your neighbor. Of course with you and Jed already knowing each other I'm sure he wanted to see how you were doing."

Aren't you the least bit curious as to how your

brother and his family are doing? How they have been doing?

"He was glad to see me." She released a breath. "Well, I won't keep you any longer. Mr. Warner is waiting for you. Again thank you for your time, Abel. And I meant it when I told Jed you were caring." She turned and walked to her door. " 'Night, Abel. Again I appreciate everything."

" 'Night Lynne."

She leaned against the door with arms folded on her chest and allowed her eyes to follow every step that he took up the pathway. She didn't go inside until he and Samson were completely out of sight.

As she headed upstairs to the bedroom, she was determined to take a bath and try to wash away that wonderful scent of him that still lingered over her. He smelled woodsy with the aftershave he wore. It had teased her nose part of the evening. She couldn't stay awake all night thinking of that man. Yes, she needed to wash him out of her system, but how?

Abel made her feel alive inside. Franklin always made her feel inferior even in conversations. One time she thought she and Franklin would have made a great couple but that was before she really got to know his true side. Before she found out how he could break her heart.

She thought of the way Abel had mentioned dates. Why had she even thought of their times together as dates? Maybe Jed was right after all. Perhaps deep down Abel would always want to have his privacy. Stay barricaded by himself. Had she been reading too much into things? After the brief encounters with Abel the attraction she felt for him was slowly simmering.

She didn't know if it was the mountain air or what, but she was beginning to feel something strong for Abel Mason.

She lowered herself into the warm bubble-bath water.

Abel, what is it about you that intrigues me so? Even now I find it hard to get you out of my mind.

And as the tranquil bubbles relaxed her mind she wondered how life would be if she was married to a man like Abel with his dog Samson.

It was late when Abel slid under the covers. He had seen her out of the corner of his eye as he and Samson walked up the hill. What was that statement she had made? Oh yeah, she had mentioned to Jed that he was a caring man. Wonder what Jed thought of that? Wonder what Jed thought of a lot of things lately? It had been three years since he had spoken to Jed on a personal note. Just a casual wave now and then if he saw him on the street passing by, but that was about all there was between them. Even when the phone rang, he never answered any of the calls. He would love to see the boys again. And Gwen. The last he heard she was expecting a baby. At least that was what the rumors in town stirred.

So Lynne considered him caring. She was a nice person to be around. He could easily talk to her. And they enjoyed each other's company.

He rubbed his eyes then shook his head. He wouldn't allow this to happen again. It had been three years since he had been close to anyone. He didn't need someone to start interfering in his life. He had Samson and that was all that he needed.

He punched his pillow then turned in the bed. Again he couldn't get her out of his mind. Since the episode with the ladder he always saw her falling and him arriving in time to catch her. To feel her feather-light body fall into his arms. To smell her perfume, feel the softness of her hair as it lightly brushed against his face. Why couldn't he get her face out of his mind? Even Samson liked her.

Thoughts of another time and another place filled his mind. He remembered the feelings that he had held with Ilene. It was almost as if Ilene was trying to come back to him. Things like that never happened. Ilene was gone. Lynne was here. Ilene had taken that long fall. If he hadn't arrived in time, Lynne would have taken a fall. Maybe not as serious as the one Ilene had taken but still a fall that could have damaged her in some way.

Samson sure had taken a liking to her. Almost the same way as he had Ilene. Three long years and now an angel had fallen into his arms. An angel that was not soon going to find her way out of his mind.

He exhaled a breath. *Lynne Murphy, why did you have to buy that cabin? Why did you have to move next to me? I wish you would pack up and move back to where you came from.*

But as he turned off the lamp he knew he didn't mean it.

Chapter Three

It had been a week since Lynne had seen or spoken to Abel. She tried to do some illustrations on a new book that had been sent to her. This one happened to be about a dog and the more she tried to draw the dog into the story the more her mind raced to Samson then to Abel. "Ready, willing, and Abel" would always sound loudly in her mind. She wondered how they were doing. If they missed her or wanted to even see her. He must take his craft seriously to never step out of the house when he was on a project.

Once she considered sneaking up the hill just to pay Samson a visit but she didn't chance it. What if it destroyed any friendship that she chose to make with Abel? Surely he would come back around one day, if only to see if she stayed off the ladders.

She put the drawings down and stood to her feet. Maybe he would enjoy a visit after this time apart. She started to go out the door when the phone rang.

"Hello."

"Hey baby, what are you doing? I haven't heard from you in a while. Miss me?"

Wrong somebody.

"Franklin, what made you decide to call? How did you get my number?"

"Directory Assistance. Give me some credit. And like I said, haven't heard from you in a while. I wanted to make sure that you weren't still upset with me over that little tiff."

Little tiff?

"I've been busy. It takes time to get settled into a new area."

"So when are you going to invite me to visit?"

Never.

"Lynne?"

"Franklin, I told you when I left that you and I needed to go our separate ways."

"If you're still bothered by my actions, I promise it will never happen again. I'm sorry I allowed my temper to heat like that. I apologized seven times over for my behavior toward you. I am willing to change, Lynne."

"Franklin, it wasn't just your temper."

"Oh that. Hey, I wasn't trying to steal your ideas. I wasn't. You're the best artist here. I can't compete with the great Lynne Murphy."

She caught the slight touch of sarcasm in his voice.

"I hate to go now but I was about to go out the door. I've got an appointment to take care of," she lied.

"You haven't met anyone up that way to take my place?"

Actually yes. But he doesn't know I exist.

"Lynne?"

You mean like you did me? How the minute I left on the last trip I took, you immediately found another woman in the wings, after you confessed your dying love to me? Oh how she wanted to say that. It wasn't bad enough that he had stolen her designs but finding another person so fast had devastated her.

"I'm too occupied with my career now, Franklin. I tried explaining that to you."

"Yeah, you did. Tell me, did you by any chance mention anything about us to Mack?"

"Mack is my boss. We only discuss business."

"Just curious." He allowed a moment of silence to pass before them. "Look Lynne, I am sorry for the way I acted. Please believe me. As far as that other woman is concerned, it meant nothing to me."

Lynne shut her eyes then opened them. She didn't want to think about that. It was too painful. How could a man declare his undying love then the next time she was out of town, go looking for another woman?

"Franklin, I really have to go."

"Sure. Talk to you later. Give me a call when you have the time."

"Okay. 'Bye, Franklin."

" 'Bye."

Lynne slammed the phone down on the hook then headed for the door. She wished Franklin had never found out her phone number. She should have requested an unlisted number. She closed the door and started running. She wanted to get the bad feelings out of her head that she was feeling. And she wanted to see Abel and Samson. If only Abel had been the one to call. If only . . .

*   *   *

Abel waited until Samson finished the dog bone then stood to his feet.

"Well, boy, I think I'm going to have to go into town and see Gene about the rest of those supplies. I suppose that I could ask Lynne if I could borrow her truck. She did offer. I need to get mine running again."

Samson sat up, barked, and wagged his tail.

"Yeah, I suspect you miss her too. Well, come on, let's go pay her a visit. But I'll tell you a secret—I really don't know what I'm doing. Remember I said after Ilene, no woman will ever be a part of my life again?" He patted Samson on his back. "Yeah, I guess in a way I'm eating my words. There's just something about Lynne that I miss."

Samson padded down the hill with Abel trailing. A few moments later, Abel started whistling a happy tune. He didn't know why he was so happy today. He just was. Perhaps because he was going to go see the lovely woman who felt so right when she fell into his arms that day. He was halfway down the path when he thought he heard something.

Lynne didn't care where she was running. She wanted to cleanse her mind of Franklin. When she moved away she was sure that he would stay out of her life forever. But no, he had to call. And for certain he would make another call and another. Franklin was just that way. He didn't take no for an answer. And yes she had told Mack about him. But she wasn't about to inform Franklin.

"Oh, why did that man have to call here?" she echoed out loud.

Lynne never saw the broken branch of the tree or the medium-size rock as she flipped and stumbled over facedown on the gravel pathway. She was groaning slightly when Samson raced to her.

He started barking then lightly nudged her.

"Samson?" She rolled over to her side as Abel hurried to her side and knelt down.

"Lynne? Are you all right? What happened? What were you doing out this way?"

His strong hands cradled her head as he gazed at the scrape on the side of her face. Her forehead had landed into a pile of rocks.

"I was trying to work off some frustration by running. I guess my mind was preoccupied."

"Can you walk? Here, let me help you stand."

Abel lifted her to her feet. But when she applied some pressure to her left foot it ached.

"Ouch. I think that I may have turned my ankle. Do you have time to help me back to my cabin?"

He swung her in his arms before she finished the question. "I think I might better take you into the clinic."

"Abel, I'm fine really."

"We aren't taking any chances. Secure your arms around my neck."

"I don't want to be a bother."

"Do it, Lynne."

She obeyed his husky voice.

Two hours later they were back inside the cabin. Abel placed her on the sofa, then put a pillow under her foot.

"You heard the doctor, you are to stay off this foot.

It is only a sprain but it could turn serious." He allowed a finger to touch the bottom of her chin while turning her face to look at the small scrape. "Did it hurt when he cleaned it?"

"Sort of stung."

"Can I get you anything?" he asked, then moved his finger away from her face.

Put your hand near my face again. The touch felt warm.

"You've done enough already. You never mentioned how you stumbled upon me."

"I was going to ask could I borrow your truck. I needed to go see Gene about the other items I needed for the project I'm working on. But when I saw you on the ground like that my mind was more concerned over you."

"Seems like you're always coming to my rescue. You can use the truck. Why don't you take it now and go get the supplies?"

"If I leave now, you'll get up and start moving."

"No. I'll stay right here until you return. Just make sure the phone is by me and hand me a bottle of water out of the refrigerator."

He rubbed his chin.

"Abel, you can trust me. Don't give me that look."

"All right. But if I find out . . ."

"Scout's honor. Now go before it gets dark."

"Samson will stay here."

"He could come inside."

"No. He loves the outdoors. He stays by the front porch door."

"Guarding me no doubt."

"Correct, Miss Murphy. I won't be gone long. Do you like burgers and shakes?"

"Yes."

"I'll bring us some dinner."

"Sounds good."

"Lynne, you never told me why you were so frustrated that you had to go running."

She looked at the phone remembering the man who called.

"Just a deadline I'm working on. I want the drawings to be perfect," she lied innocently.

He eyed the drawings that were displayed on the coffee table. They all looked perfect in his eyes. He leaned over and feathered her forehead with a kiss.

"I won't be gone long."

Lynne reclined on the sofa and waited patiently for his return. He had carried her in his arms all the way to the truck then drove to the clinic. Then when they arrived back at the cabin he had carried her inside and placed her lovingly on the sofa. And when he left he had feathered a kiss on her forehead. The thoughts ran through her mind. She needed to tell Jed just how dear and caring his brother was. She looked at the time. She could call him now and talk to him while he was still at work.

"I appreciate you telling me this, Lynne. You really should be more careful on those trails and pathways," Jed said after Lynne finished.

"I had something on my mind."

"No doubt Abel."

"Not really. Someone from back home had phoned. I didn't much care for the conversation."

"Bad news?"

"Not the way you think. You know Abel said he would bring us a burger and shake back when he returned."

"Lynne, I wouldn't stake too much stock in all of this. You only just met Abel. He may be caring and showing you a good deal of concern now but he's never going to commit to anything. Trust me, I know."

"So he's only seeing me as a weak female? A neighbor who has no one to take care of her?"

"I didn't voice that."

"You didn't have to. I can almost see your expressions too. Tell you what, the holidays are coming up. Why don't you set an extra plate? I'll make sure Abel attends this year."

Silence.

"I'll tell Gwen to set the extra place for you. She's always had a setting for Abel just in case he had a change of heart. Been doing that for the past three years. She won't give up on the man."

"And neither will I. I'll talk to you later, Jed."

"Just be careful. The next accident might land you in the hospital."

"Thanks Jed. See you later." She placed the phone back on the cradle.

Resting her head against the cushion on the sofa, she smiled. If she played her cards right, Abel would indeed be at that dinner making up with his brother.

Lynne was watching a movie when Abel returned.

"Here you go, burgers, fries, and chocolate shakes. I failed to ask what kind you preferred. But something told me that you probably loved chocolate."

"Something told you right."

"Did you move from that spot?"

"Nope. Didn't even go to take a bathroom break."

"Could you use one?"

"Yes. I need to wash my hands too."

He lifted her to her feet. "Hold on to me for support."

"Abel, it's not that bad. Only a sprain."

"Doc said stay off of it. Come on. Food is already getting cold."

She pasted a smile on her face as he led her to the downstairs bathroom.

"I'll be right outside. And after you eat, you should get in that hot tub. It will relax your muscles."

Lynne followed his orders. They shared a fast-food dinner then he started some water in the hot tub. When it was ready he helped her to the room.

"When you get in the water let me know. I'm going to go unload the truck and I'll be right back. Think you'll be okay while I'm gone?"

"I will be most careful."

"I'm taking Samson with me. We won't be gone long."

Lynne allowed the motion of the water to soothe her muscles. She couldn't make it out. Why was Abel being so kind to her? For a week there had been no communication between the two and now it was as if they were carrying on a boyfriend/girlfriend relationship. No, she just couldn't make it out. Of course she didn't mind at all. Abel made her feel important. Made her feel like a soft female who needed looking after. She could really get used to having him around permanently. For a good while she had longed to find someone to marry and have children with. Someone to share time with. Abel Mason was looking better every day in her mind.

An hour later Abel returned. Lynne was getting out of the hot tub and slipping on some green cotton pajamas. There was a tap at the door.

"Yes Abel. I'm almost ready. Wait one minute."

"Okay."

She looked in the mirror then at the pajamas. They were thick. She didn't slip on the robe, just draped it over her arm. As she opened the door he was leaning against the wall. She couldn't help but notice the half smile on his lips and those glistening blue eyes of his.

"You look refreshed. Hold onto my arm again." He stretched out his arm and wrapped it around her small waist. "I started a fire. I thought we could enjoy some warmth and easy conversation before you turned in."

Warmth? She was already feeling it from her head to her toes. Not just with that half smile of his but his hand wrapped around her waist was stirring those heartstrings again.

"Sounds nice. We could have a cup of hot cocoa as well."

"One step ahead of you. Just have to pour it in the cups."

"You've been busy, Abel."

She stretched out on the sofa and spread the robe over her. "Did you get everything done that needed to be done?" she asked as he handed her a cup of cocoa.

"I did. I appreciate the use of the truck." He sat across from her on the hassock by the fire.

"Anytime."

"You let any stranger use that truck?" He took a sip of the cocoa.

"No. You're the first. And you were no stranger. You caught me from falling and you've been cordial to me ever since I arrived. That is why I told you that you were welcome to use it anytime." *And you're Jed's brother.*

"Well, I did sweep it out after I unloaded it. Left it clean inside as well. I've got an old truck but it needs some work. Like I told you the day in the supermarket, I'm so close to town that I normally hike." He shook his head. "I never anticipated a petite little gal like yourself to be able to maneuver that Dodge Ram but you showed me that day we came home with the groceries that you can handle her pretty good."

"Yes I can. Just can't stay atop ladders or watch where I'm running." They both laughed and she wondered how long it had been since he had laughed. She finished the last of her cocoa and set the cup on the coffee table.

Silence passed between them for a few minutes. Abel put another log on the fire then leaned back on his heels. He looked into her eyes.

"You know about me, don't you?"

"Excuse me?"

"I'm no fool, Lynne. I figured that night when you were speaking of Jed that he had told you everything about me. Let me guess, he told you to stay clear of me. That I wasn't the right person to be around."

She swallowed, then cast her eyes to the floor, then gazed into the fire. "I decide who I will stay away from, Abel. Like I have mentioned, I told Jed that you were a caring man. I meant it. I usually know when I can trust someone."

"You feel like you can trust me?"

"Absolutely."

She wanted to tell him how she had missed him the whole week but she didn't want to spoil the moment.

"Jed mention about family?"

"He did."

Abel stood to his feet then finished the cocoa in the cup. After sitting the empty cup down he issued a breath.

"You must know Jed quite well for him to open up to you."

"I rented this cabin many times before I decided to buy it. I would visit with Jed, Gwen, and the boys. He knows the Parkinsons pretty well. They were all like family to me."

"Lynne, don't be a go-between where my brother and his family are concerned. It won't work. If you want to be my friend then leave things as they are."

"Isn't that a bit irrational? I mean, he's your flesh and blood. He wants to get back with you."

"Lynne, don't. You don't know what is going on around here."

"I know enough to know that man is hurting. The boys want to see their uncle again. And Gwen . . ."

"What about Gwen?" He shook his leg out, easing an oncoming cramp before it grew worse.

"Gwen is expecting another child. Jed said a girl this time." She leaned upward on the sofa. "Don't you understand the holidays are coming up? They want you to be there with them. Gwen sets a place for you every year. Life is too short to keep things bottled inside, Abel. Not only that—Gwen may have the baby before the holidays. You should be a part of that blessed event."

"Lynne, I told you stay out of it. Now I've come to your rescue twice now. I told you if you want my friendship that you will drop this." He paced the length of the fireplace. "You talk about me getting with my family. Tell me why you moved down here. Why did you leave your family?"

"New York was where I lived. Where I worked. I didn't say I left any family behind."

"They must be somewhere. They will be expecting you during the holidays."

"This isn't about me. It concerns you and Jed. I like him. I don't like to see families split. Ilene has been gone for three years. You need support from your family, Abel."

Fire burned in his eyes. She saw it and clamped her mouth shut. She didn't mean for those words to stumble off her tongue. Abel zoomed over to her, lifted her, then carried her up the stairs. He stood her down until the covers were turned down then he placed her on the bed. He pulled the covers up toward her neck.

"I don't ever want to hear about Ilene. This doesn't concern you, Lynne. You've never lost anyone like I have. It's only Samson and me now. I'll never allow my heart to get close to anyone again. Do you hear me?"

She slowly nodded. So much for the warmth she was feeling for him. But he had mentioned friendship.

"As far as holidays, they are just another day, nothing more. Now go to sleep, you need your rest. If you need a pain pill just call me. I'm staying on your sofa tonight. Don't let me hear you stirring this house tonight. You call me if you need something."

"I never asked you to stay. I can get along fine."

"I'm looking after you as a friend and that's all there is to it."

"Being a Good Samaritan to a friend in need? Or perhaps a clumsy woman?"

"Maybe a little of both."

"I can take care of myself, Abel. I don't need your pampering." But as the words fell from her lips, she knew it was a lie. She was enjoying his pampering.

He turned to leave when she stopped him.

"Abel, I'm sorry if I upset you. As for my family, I have none. I'm an orphan. I was never adopted by anyone. I don't know anything about my parents, if they are dead or alive. I never bothered checking into my past. No one told me if I was just dropped off at the orphanage or what. This is my first real home. One day I want to marry and have a husband and children of my own.

"As for holidays, mine have been spent with large crowds of orphaned children or either at the shelters during that time of the year. Since I've grown up, I visit with others who don't have families. When I heard Jed mention his brother, it made me wish that I had that closeness that your brother wants to regain with you. I can't promise you that I won't bring it up again, so if you want to renounce that friendship between us now, I'll understand."

His eyes swept her form as it lay under the covers. Why was her lovely face slowly entering his mind, erasing Ilene's? Why couldn't he just walk away from her? Turn his back and go out that door back to the life he had before she fell in his arms? He stepped back to the bed leaned over and softly kissed her scratched cheek.

"Go to sleep, Lynne." He stood straight. "Please. I haven't pampered anyone in a long time. Let me take care of you tonight."

She wanted to tell him she didn't need his help. She had taken care of herself all these years. Why start now with his help? But as the words drummed in her mind, her heart told her to let him stay.

She rolled to her side and tried to shut her eyes.

"Good night, Lynne."

" 'Night, Abel."

It seemed that was all they were doing again was telling each other good night. Yet this time he feathered her with a soft kiss from his lips. Didn't he realize how that was affecting her? Friendship? She couldn't just have friendship with this man. Could it be possible to fall in love with a man in so short a time? But she was. A man who still carried his buried wife in his heart. *Oh Abel, what am I going to do?*

Chapter Four

Lynne rolled over onto her back and halfway opened her eyes. She stretched her arms. What was that aroma? It smelled like eggs and bacon frying. But who? Oh yes, Abel had said that he was going to be spending the night on the sofa. Was he preparing breakfast? She sat upright then swung her legs over the bed. She started to stand when she felt a twist of pain rush up her leg.

"Ouch," she said lightly. She didn't think the fall had been that hard when she fell but her run had been intense. All due to the phone call with Franklin.

Abel removed the omelets from the frying pan, then turned off the stove. He thought he heard something coming from upstairs. In three strides he was across the room and heading up the stairs.

"I thought I heard movement. Lynne, what did I tell you last night?"

She steadied herself and eyed him casually. His hair was combed neatly. He was wearing the same clothes from the night before but he looked good. She adjusted the sleeve of her pajama top then smoothed her hand through her hair. She knew she looked a mess when she awoke each morning but he was standing there admiring her as if she was a pretty sight to behold.

"You told me not to stir during the night. By the look of things, it is morning." She threw a smile his way.

Her hair was tossed and flowing halfway off her shoulder and lying near the front of her neck. To Abel she was very pretty when she awoke.

"Yeah, I guess that I did say during the night. Did I hear you cry out?"

"It was a faint ouch. I didn't realize that I would be sore this morning. I didn't know that I had fallen that hard."

"You did plunge headlong into some rocks and the gravel wasn't soft when you plastered on it. Let me take a look at that cheek." He started walking directly to her.

No, Abel, I haven't brushed my teeth yet. I need to freshen up. You know, comb my hair? But it was too late—he was standing right in front of her as his hand palmed the side of her cheek.

"A slight coloring but not too much. There are a few little lines of the scrape showing. Does it hurt to stand on your foot?" He knelt down and lifted her foot. She braced one hand on his shoulder to balance her. "I think that you might ought to stay off it one more day. I'll call the doc to let him know how you did during the night. Were you headed to the bathroom?" He asked as he placed her foot back to the floor and stood upright.

Lynne stood frozen. Just the simple touch of his hand on her cheek and foot had sent embers of fire through her.

"Lynne?"

"Sorry. Yes, I was headed that way."

"Go on. I'll wait here for you then help you down the stairs."

"Abel, I can—"

He raised an index finger. "No arguments."

"All right. I'll try to hurry.",

"Don't rush. I have the omelets wrapped in foil staying hot for us."

Omelets, he had made omelets.

Lynne hurried and freshened up. She wished she hadn't looked such a mess when he first saw her but he didn't appear too disappointed in her. She brushed through her hair, fluffed it, ran the toothbrush over her teeth, then sprayed on some deodorant before heading out the door.

"You didn't have to make my bed. I could have done that."

"Just trying to help. Ready to eat?"

"Yes. The aroma drifted up here. Smells good."

She took hold of his arm but he only swung her in his arms and started down the steps. "I don't think that you need to take the steps. Do you mind?"

Heavens no. "No. I just don't want you to hurt your back."

"As light as you are?" He landed her lightly on one of the barstools. "Now if you eat all your food I'll let you see Samson."

He handed her the omelet with a glass of orange juice.

"Thank you."

He sat across from her and poured two cups of coffee. "I hope you like bacon and cheese omelets."

"Yes. This is great. Did you use some of the spices?"

"Yes. But please don't ask me what kind. I went crazy with your spice rack."

"Told you different blends of spices really zest up foods." She forked some of the omelet into her mouth then talked over the food. "So, Abel, did you sleep well enough on the sofa?"

"I did. It is comfortable."

"I should have informed you that it had a sleeper bed inside. You could have opened it up. I had extra sheets."

"Nah, it was fine the way it was." He finished one cup of coffee then poured another. He gestured the pot to Lynne.

"No, one is enough for me. I don't drink that much. Just keep the pot for guests." She watched as he ate the omelet.

He caught her staring at him. "Lynne, something wrong?"

"I just noticed after all this time that you are left-handed. I didn't even pay attention to that in all the times we have shared a meal."

"Probably because I use both hands. I am left-handed but I broke my left arm at one time all the way down to part of my hand. Couldn't use it to write or do much of anything so I learned from my right hand for almost three months."

"Was it hard?"

"At first yes. It was like learning all over when

you're a young child. But I kept practicing until I finally got the knack of it."

"Guess it can be helpful being able to use both hands."

"It does have its advantages." He pushed his plate aside. "Will you be okay while I go work on my project?"

She took the last bite then wiped the corner of her mouth with the napkin. "Abel, I told you already. You don't have to house-sit me. I'll stay off my foot. I'm going to go change clothes and spend the morning watching a little television then work on my drawings."

"I want to watch over you until I know that ankle is fine. Why don't you just lounge around in your pajamas today? I can put a bucket with ice near you to keep your water cool. At lunchtime I'll break and bring you a sandwich."

She rubbed her stomach. "I doubt I will want any lunch. This was filling. I won't be hungry until dinner."

"Okay. I'll do these dishes then head out."

"Why don't we just rinse them off and put them in the dishwasher?"

He knitted his eyebrows together watching her finish the glass of orange juice. "Why don't we?"

Abel helped her to the sofa. He wouldn't allow her to touch one dish. She watched how he put the dishes away and cleared the counter. He seemed to fit in so well. He had said friends last night. Well if it was only friends, then that was better than nothing.

"Hey, you forgot to let me see Samson and I ate all my food, mister."

"I didn't forget. Let me wash this frying pan and you can see him."

There was the sound of a car. Abel peeped out the kitchen window as the man was getting out of the car heading to the front door. He shook his head. Trapped with no place to go.

"Abel, someone's out there."

"Yeah," he said, disgusted. He walked around and opened the door before the hand even knocked.

"Oh, Abel, I didn't expect—"

Lynne couldn't tell which of the two brothers was more shocked to see the other. Jed or Abel. Jed was carrying a box of chocolates. Abel opened the door wide then swung back around to the other side of the counter toward the sink.

"Jed, good morning. What brings you out this way?" Lynne inquired.

He eyed the room and Lynne sitting on the sofa in pajamas with foot propped up. He remembered the fall but didn't let on he knew.

"Please come in. I had a fall yesterday and sprained my ankle when I was running." She winked without Abel seeing her. "Abel was kind enough to spot me and take me to the clinic. The doc said to stay off the ankle. Abel offered to prepare me an omelet this morning. In fact he has been taking care of me since the accident. Would you care for anything? A cup of coffee?"

Jed watched as Abel washed the frying pan then placed it in the drainer. "No, I just finished with Gwen and the boys." So Abel was still hanging around. Maybe that was a good sign after all. He handed

Lynne the box. "Gwen wanted you to have this. She remembered how you loved chocolates and today."

Abel looked over at her. *Today?*

"She remembered it was your birthday. The boys wanted to give you something too. They're out in the—"

It was too late; they were bouncing in the door. "Daddy, Daddy," they both said together.

"I asked you boys—"

"But Daddy," six-year-old Eric prompted. "Samson is here. We saw him. He is bigger now, Daddy."

"Yeah, Daddy," Brad said. "That has to mean that Uncle Abel is nearby. He wouldn't leave Samson by himself."

Abel watched how bubbly the boys were. They had yet to notice him in the kitchen area behind the counter. Eric had grown so much in the three years. His hair was dark brown just like Gwen's. And little Brad. How long had it been? He had to be seven now. Had they flourished that much in three years? Lynne watched as Abel swept his eyes over them.

"Aunt Lynne, what happened to your foot? Why is it propped up on the pillow?" Eric asked, switching the chat to her.

Abel noticed how he called her aunt.

"I fell running yesterday. I only turned it. Nothing to worry about."

He handed her a flower. "This is from me and Brad. We know you love roses. Happy Birthday!"

"Yes, Happy Birthday!" Brad chimed in.

They each gave her a hug.

"Thank you, boys. I'll place this in water and think of you every time I see it."

"Why is Samson here, Aunt Lynne? Have you seen Uncle Abel? He wouldn't leave Samson all alone." It was Eric asking.

"No, he—"

Brad was the first to turn his head and see him. "Uncle Abel!" A smile as wide at the grand ol' Mississippi River spanned his lips. He ran to him followed by Eric. They both buried their arms around him.

"Uncle Abel," Eric beamed.

Abel couldn't help himself. He knelt down leaning on his heels and hugged them both tightly. Nothing was said for a couple of minutes. Jed shrugged his shoulders then wiped his eyes. Lynne had a few tears misting in her eyes too. A moment later Abel stood up. Each boy had a hold of his hand.

"Daddy, why didn't you tell us that Uncle Abel was going to be here for Aunt Lynne's birthday?" Brad asked.

But it was Abel who answered. "Your dad didn't know that I was here, boys."

"Did you want it to be a surprise?" Eric asked, displaying his teeth. One of the front ones was missing.

It made Abel realize how much he had really missed not spending time with the boys. Ilene would have scolded him dearly for that. He had been a rotten uncle all these years not to mention brother. He wanted to cry but not in front of Jed.

"Boys, we need to go. We promised your mother we would hurry back. You never know when your little sister might decide to arrive early."

Abel locked eyes with Jed but said nothing. Gwen was going to have a little girl. Jed needed to be home with her now. What if something happened this close to her due date? Lynne saw the concerned look dance over Abel's face. She covered her hand halfway over her mouth trying to stay calm. She knew the tears would rush out any minute.

"Promise you will come see us, Uncle Abel?" Brad mentioned. "Mommy is going to have a bigger turkey this year. She always sets a place for you. Then she tells us that you couldn't make it cause you had to work. No one should have to work on turkey day. And we are going to have a little sister. You have to come see her. She said she was going to name the baby after Aunt Ilene. That way you would have to come to visit with us."

Liquid misted in Abel's eyes. "Boys, you should go with your dad now. Your mom needs you with her."

"But you haven't promised, Uncle Abel." It was Eric reminding.

"I will see what I can do. I'm busy making some woodwork at the moment. I'll try. I don't want to make a promise. If I can't make it then it would be bad luck."

"All right. That will have to do," Eric said sadly. He hugged him once more.

Brad hugged him next. "We love you, Uncle Abel." The boys gave Lynne a huge hug and kiss.

"The candy is from us too, Aunt Lynne," Eric said.

"Thank you boys. I will enjoy every bite."

Brad pulled out a drawing from behind a chair. "What's this, Aunt Lynne?" he asked while handing it to her. "It looks like Samson and Uncle Abel."

Abel eyed the drawing as well as Jed.

"It was a gift that I was going to surprise your Uncle Abel with."

"Guess it's not much of a surprise now," Jed stated.

"That's all right. I'm sure when I hand it to Abel that he will still act surprised." She forced a smile toward Abel, wondering what was registering in his head right now.

"Come on boys," Jed said. "I don't want to worry your mom. Lynne, Happy Birthday, we'll keep in touch. Gwen said that she would phone you later today."

"Thanks, Jed."

The boys cast a wave to Abel who returned one. Jed looked his way. " 'Bye brother. Hope you are doing well."

"I'm doing fine," Abel said as his voice choked. "Jed, you've got a fine set of boys there. They sure have grown." He cleared his throat. The lump was rising higher.

"They've missed you, Abel. We all have," Jed said before going out the door.

Lynne watched them leave. Abel stood with arms crossed. He noticed that Lynne was still holding the drawing in her hand.

When they heard the car drive away his eyes linked with hers. Now that they were alone she wished that she were a fly so that she could buzz out of the room. Abel's eyes seemed to be full of sparks and it sure wasn't the good kind that made you tingle all the way down to your toes. It had been an awkward moment but both brothers had handled it well.

Chapter Five

Lynne raised her palms in the air. "Now before you blow this out of proportion and start telling me that I was interfering, I had no idea that Jed was coming by today. And never did he suspect you to be here doing dishes in my kitchen. This is something they do for me whenever I come up to visit."

"Which is?"

"I come every end of October to stay in the cabin. Well, I have for the last three years. It's on record that I stay at this cabin for a weekend. That was the only time that I could get off. I enjoy the color changing in the leaves. I got to talking to Jed when I first rented the place. Gwen and the boys were there. They were like family to me after a while. Remember I never had one. It felt good having that closeness to people that made me feel special. And Gwen has that way of doing so."

He wouldn't argue there. Gwen always had a way in making a person feel wanted. Lynne ached for a

family. He could tell by her words. No father, no
mother. At least he and Jed had been blessed with
parents. They had been adults when their parents had
been killed. Just an unexpected car accident that had
claimed both their lives. Jed had Gwen to be there to
offer solace and at the time he had Ilene near for him.

But whom had Lynne cuddled up to all these years?
Who had she shared her birthdays and holidays with?
Large groups of people he recalled she mentioned during the holidays, but what about her birthday? Wasn't
there a special person in her life that she dated or cared
enough to think of her? Coming from New York there
must have been people that she worked with. Not only
was she an attractive young woman, she was warm
and loving. Who wouldn't want to cuddle up with her?
Those button eyes of hers were drawing him in over
his head.

*Say something, Abel. Don't just stand there. My pa-
tience grows thin after a while.*

"Yeah, it was just a coincidence. I was surprised
how much the boys had grown."

"I've seen the change each time I came down to
visit."

"I notice they referred to you as Aunt Lynne."

"Does that bother you?"

"Should it?"

"I wouldn't want it to. Brad asked could they call
me that. I had no objections. Like I said it makes me
feel like family."

He leaned back on his heels. "You don't have anyone in New York that you are fond of? Friends? I
know you said no family."

"A boss. A couple of people I saw when I was

working on my projects. It was all mostly work with me."

He bit on his lower lip. "No male friends?"

Her eyes met with his, locking them together. She didn't want him to know about Franklin. She was never serious about him. He may have thought they were serious material but Franklin's domineering ways make her feel a bit frightened to even be in the same room with him. Abel was so much different from Franklin. Even his scolding and mention of staying out of his family wasn't spoken in harsh tone to her. Maybe a bit frosty at times but never as austere as Franklin.

"Lynne?"

"I told you, Abel. Do I have to continue explaining that I have been almost a loner all my life?" She couldn't bring herself to inform him of Franklin. He had stolen her ideas so many times that she had to get away from him. From now on she went through Mack. Only Mack. He promised her that he would intercept all her drawings. Her ideas would never fall into the hands of Franklin again.

She lowered her eyes to the drawing. Abel carefully removed it from her hands.

"You did this without me or Samson posing?"

"Yes. From memory. Do you like it?"

He gave a closer look at the drawing. It was identical to him and Samson. "You do excellent work." He rubbed his chin. He felt the stubble. He hadn't had a chance to shave this morning. "I knew the other illustrations were good but this is great, Lynne. You should consider opening a shop in downtown Gatlinburg and doing sketches of people. We get a lot of tourists who would love to have their portraits done."

"I suppose it would give me something to think about."

"When did you do this?"

"The night you brought me the stew. I wanted to give you an appreciation of thanks."

"You had thanked me enough, Lynne."

"I wanted to give you something that you could remember me by."

"Why haven't you given it to me?"

"I didn't know if you would think I was . . . what I mean is, some men might think a woman was pushing for more by giving gifts."

"I'm not *some* men." His tone was a bit sharp then he flashed a smile her way.

"You're welcome to take it with you."

"Thank you. I'll get a frame and hang it over the fireplace." He swept his eyes over her once more as a thought ran through his mind. "I didn't get a chance to pick up a few extra items that I need for the wood. Could I borrow the truck for a few minutes?"

"Abel, you can always borrow it when you need it. I told you that."

"I like to ask first. Need to get anything before I head out?"

"You haven't allowed me to see Samson."

He pulled her to her feet and helped her to the front porch. "There you go. Sit in the rocker and spend a few minutes with Samson. I need to make one phone call before I leave."

Abel made sure she was out of hearing range. He quickly dialed the number. "This is Abel. I need to come by for a few minutes. I'm on my way now." He placed the phone back to the cradle. Closing his eyes for a moment, he drew a breath. He hoped that he was doing the right thing. Why had Lynne Murphy come into his life, upsetting everything? He was doing just fine until that pretty petite woman had fallen into his arms. Now Jed and the boys had arrived in a halfway friendly reunion and the boys were melting his heart.

What was said about the baby? Oh yes, Gwen was naming the baby girl Ilene, then maybe Abel would come around. *Stop it.* Why couldn't he make his heart stop melting? Yes, he could hear Ilene scolding him good for not being with his family these last three years. He saw Lynne slowly coming inside.

"Sorry, I need to go to the bathroom. All that juice and the cup of coffee this morning. I can make it."

He watched her slowly pad barefooted to the bathroom. A few minutes later she came out. He was holding the drawing in his hand while he stood by the front door.

"I've got some ice in a bowl with your bottled water. Your drawing supplies are on the coffee table along with the remote to the television. I put some extra cushions around the sofa for you. Let me make sure that you get situated."

He led her over to the sofa and stopped.

"Do you think you'll need anything else?"

"No, this is all I'll need, Abel. You've been too generous."

"I won't be gone too long. I'll take the truck to the house to unload the other stuff I'm picking up. I'll give you a call when I return. Samson has food and water on the front porch. He'll let you know if he sees anyone. I'm locking the door."

"Okay Abel. I'll stay off my foot. Did you call the doctor? You said you were going to call."

"I didn't get an answer," he lied. He hated doing that to her. "I think that I'll go by there and let him know how you are doing." He continued to look down into those button eyes of hers. She was so pretty. He wondered what it would feel like to run a finger through that thick bouncy hair. It had been a long time since he had last felt a woman's hair.

Lynne couldn't make out his expression. Why was he staring at her that way? His blue eyes were so hypnotic. She was blown away by his next move. With one sweeping movement, he had his lips firmly on hers, kissing her slowly. A minute later he broke the kiss then sat her on the sofa.

"Why did you have to come here, Lynne Murphy? Why?" He turned and marched out the door.

Abel nursed the cup of coffee that Gwen had poured him. Why did he feel nervous being here? She was his sister-in-law. It had been good to enter the house and see everything the same. To give Gwen a hug had felt even greater.

Gwen sat next to him and gently touched his hand. "There is no need for you to feel uncomfortable. This is part of your home too."

"I had to see you after Jed and the boys came by this morning. They were headed back this way. Why aren't they here for you now?"

"He called and said he had to go by the office after he dropped the boys off at school. They ran late this morning because Brad had to go get a shot. Eric went along for the ride. The teachers said they wouldn't miss any work. They are doing great in school."

"I wondered why they dropped by the cabin so early."

"Eric wanted to give Lynne her rose first thing."

"She was pleased with it and the box of chocolates. It was as if no one else remembers her birthday."

"She doesn't have anyone else, Abel."

He gulped the coffee down then placed the cup on the coaster. "You know when Jed left he mentioned that he needed to return to you because of the baby."

Gwen gloved her hand in his. "Abel, I'm fine. I urged Jed to finish with what he needed to get done. When the baby does arrive he'll be busy lending both hands around here." She rubbed her free hand over her stomach, then took his hand and placed it there. "I hope you don't mind that I chose to name the baby after Ilene. I suppose that I should have asked your permission first."

He rubbed his hand over her stomach then let it rest.

"Gwen, I can't tell you what you can or cannot name the baby."

"I didn't want you to feel uncomfortable if you come around and hear me calling her Ilene."

He removed his hand then lowered his head toward the floor. He inhaled a breath then leaned upward. "I think Ilene would be honored that you named your girl after her. And no, Gwen, it will not bother me. It will be like her memory being passed down." He cupped her hand in his then bestowed a kiss on it.

No sooner had he kissed her hand, his thoughts ran to Lynne. He had firmly kissed her before he marched out of the cabin. Just grabbed her shoulders then pressed his lips to hers and kissed her. The question— oh no, the question. What would she think about that question? The kiss most likely surprised her, but that question. He needed to tell her that he didn't intend for it to be hurtful.

"Abel, you okay?"

"Just thinking."

"About Ilene or Lynne?"

His eyes darted to hers. "Am I that transparent?"

"You look like someone who is possibly falling in love again."

He stood to his feet. "No. That is one thing that I will never do again."

"Never say never," she said, rising from the sofa. "I think you like Lynne more than you are willing to say."

"I don't know her that well."

"You know her enough to care from what I've heard."

Abel raked a hand through his hair then stepped over to the fireplace. "She's only a friend. Nothing more."

"But you came over to ask something about her."

"I wanted to know what kind of cake she preferred. Her favorite color. I thought that I might even buy her a dozen roses. This is a young girl who has been deprived of things. Well, not deprived."

"I understand. Family things. You want to pamper her, don't you Abel? Make her feel like someone does care enough to give her things that she has missed in life."

Gwen could always read him so well. Even better than Ilene could.

He paced the room then stopped. "I don't understand why I am even doing this. Ever since she fell into my arms that day things have spun in my head. Then when I saw her sprawled on the ground my head spun more. If you could have seen how she spoke about you and Jed. How I should share the holidays with you. Of course I set her straight. Told her to not interfere if she wanted to be my friend. Wanted to know why she was not near her family."

"And that's when she told you she was an orphan?"

"She mentioned it later. You know she spends her Thanksgiving at the shelters helping out?" Gwen nodded. A few tears misted in his eyes. "What is happening to me, Gwen? Ilene has only been gone for three years. I promised her that no one would take her place. Then this Lynne Murphy has to buy that cabin. Has to start melting my heart."

"You're discovering that you are human. Do you think that Ilene wanted you to pine away in that cabin of yours? She would want you to go on living. Some people don't even wait three years. If it had been Jed, I don't know how I would act. I never want another man to be with me and the boys . . . and soon to be girl." She lightly smiled. "But sometimes things happen in our lives that we can't control. And I know that I wouldn't want Jed to be lonely all his life if I were to go before him. I've heard it affects men worse. Sometimes they need another female in their life for companionship, for warmth. To be there for them. Sort of like a helpmate."

She edged over to the fireplace. Her hand rested on his arm.

"If you are falling in love with Lynne, I don't think that you could find a finer young woman. Ilene would even be happy that you found someone like her. But Abel, never think that another woman is taking Ilene's place. No one can take the place of a loved one once they are gone. Every person is unique. If you chose to be with Lynne things would be different with her. Just remember that. And don't shut her out."

"I told her that we were friends." Abel could stand it no longer. The liquid misted heavily in his eyes. He threw himself in Gwen's arms and let three long years explode in a few short minutes of tears.

Chapter Six

Lynne set the drawing down and reclined her head to the pillow. She had watched a little television but the only scene that continued to play in her mind was the kiss. She could still feel Abel's strong hands cup her shoulders as he planted his lips firmly over hers, kissing her in such a brushing way that sent heated flames down to her bare feet. Whew—what had that one kiss meant? But his question afterwards. Did he mean he hated her living next door? Surely not by the touch of that kiss. But he had asked why.

She propped her foot higher on the cushion. She wasn't that bad off for him to continue staying here pampering her. It wasn't like he owed her anything. She sat up and stretched her arms. She needed a break. All she could think of was that kiss. She even felt the slight stubble where he hadn't shaved. His lips had tasted rich.

"Okay Lynne, stop it. The kiss was no doubt a birthday kiss and instead of wishing you a happy birthday he wanted to know why you had to come here." She stood to her feet wondering what Samson was doing.

Easing the door open, she spotted the squirrel perched on the rail and Samson reclining near the rocker. She padded outside and slipped into the rocker.

"I see the two of you have finally met. I'm surprised at you Samson. Most dogs are out chasing squirrels. I guess the two of you have become friends. Yeah, friends like me and Abel."

Samson moved to her side then laid his head in her lap. She knew she wasn't supposed to be outside but she was tired of staying inside. It was too beautiful to be trapped behind walls. She enjoyed the outdoors.

She inhaled a fresh breath then stretched her feet out, gazing at her ankle. It wasn't swollen. She had carefully watched how she walked to not cause any swelling. Her hand gently rubbed Samson's head then her fingers massaged the back of his ears.

Her mind drifted to the way that Abel had kissed her. Right smack on the lips. It was heavenly. Nothing like . . . well, she didn't wish to think about Franklin Goolsby. Sure, he had kissed her a couple of times when she thought it might have led to something, but she never felt any sensations. With Abel's kiss it was a burning flame all the way to the soles of her feet.

Samson slightly whimpered.

She wondered how it would feel to be standing in front of a preacher and hearing him pronounce the two of them as Mr. and Mrs. Abel Mason. A smile crossed her lips.

Samson let out three loud barks.

Lynne rubbed the top of his head then scratched

behind his ears. Yes, she could see the three of them together.

Samson's tail banged against the floor of the porch. Lynne laughed. It was a moment she was enjoying.

Gwen placed the phone back on the cradle. "Well, that takes care of that, Abel. All you have to do is swing by and pick up the cake and the flowers. Don't worry how things will look. I know Mabel. Her cakes are exceptional. Lynne will really love the cake. I think having chocolate inside with white and yellow roses on the outside was a good choice."

"I just found out that she loved chocolate when I took her a chocolate shake."

"With any woman, I don't think you can go wrong with chocolate. Of course with the dozen red roses you ordered, she may think you are being more than a friend now. Will that bother you?"

He chewed at his bottom lip thinking. Did it really matter? He did like Lynne. She smelled good and felt just right in his arms. And that kiss this morning.

"No it won't."

"Good for you. Now one more thing." She led him into the dining room. "This place will be set once again for you at Thanksgiving. I'm not pressuring you. I want you to know you are welcome. Whenever you want to stop over, you be sure to come no matter what. Jed and I are your family. We miss Ilene and loved her just as you did. I don't know where you got the idea that we didn't like Ilene 'cause she had Cherokee in her—"

Abel started to speak.

"No, let me finish," she said, raising a hand. "We

loved her dearly. The first minute you introduced us to her and said the two of you were going to marry, Jed and I both fell in love with her. She was a part of this family. She will always be a part of this family. She is in our hearts. The last three years have not only been hard on you but us as well."

Abel pressed his lips together. "I was so hurt after her death. Seeing her fall like that . . . well, it did something to me . . . physically and mentally. I didn't want to be around any of my family for fear that I would lose them too. I was wrong in using that excuse to not be near my family. You never held anything against Ilene. I apologize for all my actions."

"Which is why you barricaded yourself in the cabin?"

Abel nodded. He palmed his hands over his face then placed them back by his side. "After Jed and I lost our parents it was a hard blow. But losing a spouse that means so much to you . . . well, that is worse than any feeling in this world. I hope it never happens to you or Jed. I realize now that I was wrong in accusing my family in that manner. In my heart I know you accepted Ilene always." He paused, then inhaled a breath. "I am very sorry, Gwen. Until a person has walked in your shoes, one never knows what the other is really experiencing. A wise Indian told me that once."

"It's okay, Abel. You are back with us now and something tells me that things are going to start looking up for all of us." She gently patted his shoulder.

He kissed her forehead. "You're right. Thank you, Gwen. I guess you will be setting a place for Lynne since she has moved here."

"I will."

"Funny how you became friends once she started renting the cabin."

"I liked her the first time I met her. And the boys took right up with her. She has even babysat for us a few times so Jed and I could dine out." She suddenly leaned over.

"Gwen, what's wrong? Is it the baby?" Abel asked, concerned.

"I think she decided to wake up and start kicking. Ouch!" She leaned over again.

"Gwen, you're worrying me. Sit down."

Water started spraying to the floor.

"Uh-oh."

Abel swallowed. "Uh-oh what?"

"My water just broke."

"Your water?"

"Yeah. Better get me to the doctor. Give me your cell phone. While you're driving me I'll call Jed and the midwife."

"Gwen, shouldn't we wait for Jed? He could drive you. And what do you mean, midwife?"

"No. I should go now." Another sharp pain. She leaned over again. "We need to go, Abel. Once your water breaks, you shouldn't really wait. And then again it could take time. As for the midwife, this was something that I wanted with this child. I didn't want to go to a hospital. Just take me to the clinic—Doc and the midwife will have a room ready for me. Jed and I have already gone over it with them."

Abel rubbed his forehead. "Okay. When we get inside the truck we'll give Jed a call. Do you have a suitcase or something?"

"Yes, in the coat closet by the door."

Abel pulled out the small suitcase and took hold of Gwen's hand. "Are you in a lot of pain?"

"Not too much. I've got to think of the boys too. They will need to be picked up from school."

"Gwen, just worry about the baby now. I'll take care of the rest."

Abel helped her inside the truck when she moaned again.

"Another pain?"

"No. I forgot to call Lynne and wish her a Happy Birthday."

Abel shook his head then kissed her on the cheek. "Gwen, you are one in a million."

"Be sure to remind Jed."

"He already knows, I'm sure."

Lynne stood to her feet and started inside. She thought about taking a bath and changing while she was waiting for Abel. She couldn't understand why she hadn't heard from him. It seemed to be taking a long time. Surely he was all right. He did say he would call when he got to his place with the deliveries. Maybe he just got busy.

She turned and cast an eye at Samson who was stretched out enjoying the airy breeze that was slowly blowing the leaves from the trees. A smile crossed her lips. Such a lucky dog. He didn't have a care in the world. He had an owner who loved him and took good care of him. If only life were that simple. If only things were as simple as a dog's life.

Lynne stepped inside the cabin and decided to check what was on the television. She flopped on the sofa, flipping the channels. Her drawings were finished. All she had to do was mail them to Mack. Now she needed to work on the next project. That is if Mack gave all these his seal of approval. She continued to eye the phone. She reached and picked it up to see if it was working then placed it back on the hook.

"Oh, this is silly. I'm acting like a teenager in love for the very first time." *Maybe you are, Lynne.* She looked at the time. "What is keeping him?"

The phone rang.

"Hello."

"Happy Birthday, little lady."

"Mack, thank you."

"I bet you thought I forgot."

"My boss? Never."

"How are you doing? Is your day a good one?"

"Yes to both questions. I finished the drawings. Now all I have to do is zip them in the mail to you."

"I can always depend on you."

"How's your wife?"

"Much better. Thanks for asking. The surgery went well with no complications. She'll be off her foot for about six weeks, the doctor said."

"Got you doing double-time?"

"A little, but I love every minute of it. I thought I would never marry but Denise has made every minute of my life wonderful."

"I'm glad. You two make a great pair."

"So when are *you* going to tie the knot?"

"Got to find someone first."

"Not if you stay up in those hills."

"Who knows?"

"Franklin not bothering you since you left?"

"He called yesterday. Said he got my number through Information."

"I'd never give it out."

"I know."

"Lynne, you don't have to worry. You've already emailed me the designs that you are mailing to me. He won't steal any more of your ideas."

"Thanks Mack. And thank you for believing me."

"Lynne, when Franklin showed me those samples, I knew he wasn't capable of that work. I do have one thing to mention."

"Yes."

"I might need you to come back up just before Thanksgiving. One of our clients is working on a new children's book. They are eager to meet with you. Unfortunately they can only make plans just before Thanksgiving to meet with you. She wanted me to mention it to you first."

"So you do need me to come up?"

"Only if you agree. She wants to see what you can sketch the day you are here. Your work is up against another person's. She wants you to do her drawings but it seems her publicist wants her to go with another name. It could mean top dollar if we could get her publicist to go with you."

"Is she bringing her publicist?"

"Yes."

"Don't I get a name?"

"Are you sitting?"

"Yes."

"Anna Lindfors."

"You're pulling my chain."

"No."

Lynne couldn't believe her ears. "*The* Anna Lindfors wants me to do her illustrations? *Her* drawings?"

"Yes. I wish I were there to see your face now. Your enthusiasm is really coming out."

"This is something that I have always wanted."

"Don't I know." He hesitated for a moment.

Lynne could almost see his face as she had so many times. "Okay, you hesitated. What aren't you telling me? Usually you give me this big news, then you say . . . but. I bet this is one of those times."

He chuckled. "You know me so well. You have to be here before Thanksgiving to meet with her."

Lynne thought of Abel. What if she got up to New York, got snowed in, and didn't make it back for the holiday turkey? She wanted to make sure that Abel finally shared dinner with his family.

"Lynne?"

"Would I be back by Thanksgiving?"

"I don't see why not. Then again you could share it with Denise and me. Unless you have found someone?"

"I was going to share it with Gwen, Jed, and the boys."

"Oh yes, I recall you telling me about them."

"It's my first thanksgiving with a family that has made me one of theirs."

"I promise you that you will be home for Thanksgiving. But I know how important this will be for you in your career."

"So you'll call her and tell her?"

"I will. I'll get back to you. Oh, before I forget, I have to go down to Atlanta for a conference in a couple of weeks. You left some of your artwork behind that you were working on about the orphanage. I thought that I might drive by there and drop it off. You can show me that cabin you talked about so much."

"That would be nice."

"You should really consider writing the story about the orphanage, Lynne. The artwork you did really is great and you telling the story would carry much meaning."

"I have considered it, Mack. I'll give it some thought. Let me know if you can come by. I would love to see you."

"I'll keep you posted. Hope you had a good birthday."

"Yes. This was the best birthday present. Well, second best."

"What topped mine?"

"A kiss, Mack. A kiss that seared heat down to my feet."

"So you have met someone?"

"I'll talk to you later, Mack."

"This isn't fair."

"I'm hanging up, Mack."

"I'll tell Denise."

"Give her my love. 'Bye, Mack."

" 'Bye, sunshine."

Lynne stood and did a happy dance then suddenly reached for her foot as she sunk into the couch.

"Oh, oh, oh, I forgot it still smarts a bit. Anna Lindfors. I am going to draw for Anna Lindfors! Well, maybe."

She turned off the television and headed to the bathroom when the phone started ringing.

"Hello."

"Lynne."

"Abel, are you all right? Has anything happened? I was worried when you didn't call. When I checked on Samson . . ."

"Were you outside?"

"I can look out the window. I was so worried that—"

"If you're worried about your truck, it's fine."

"Truck? I'm not worried about that truck. A vehicle can be replaced. I was worried about you, silly."

"Sorry. I . . . I'm fine Lynne. It's Gwen."

"Gwen?"

"Her water broke and I drove her to the hospital."

Water broke. But how did he know? You had to be with someone. Unless she called him.

"Yes. I'm waiting on Jed to arrive. Are you okay? I didn't get to check on you. Are you hungry?"

"I'm fine. Gwen—is she in much pain?"

"She's got some pains but if they're bad she sure isn't letting on."

"I'd probably be screaming my head off."

"You, never. Lynne, about the kiss this morning."

Great—here it comes. Always the apology. Didn't mean it. It was an accident. "Yes."

"I left without telling you Happy Birthday. At the time I didn't know it was your birthday. I didn't have a gift for you. The kiss was . . . well, it was a gift."

"And the question afterward?"

"Oh Lynne, I've got to go. Here comes Jed. I'll see you in a bit. Stay off that foot."

The phone clicked.

Another unanswered question. Well, guess he would tell her when he was ready.

Thirty minutes later Lynne was out of the tub and slipping on a gown with slippers. The gown was thick enough that she wouldn't need a robe. She brushed her hair then sprayed on a bit of cologne. Abel wanted her to relax. She could still look nice to relax. Anna Lindfors. A smile laced her lips. If she couldn't have a family, her drawings were the second-best thing. She had just landed on the bottom step when the door opened.

"Aunt Lynne," Eric said, carrying in a small bag. "We get to spend the night with you. Isn't it wonderful? Mommy is having our sister and we needed a place to stay. Uncle Abel let us ride in your truck. We got to sit in the extended part. It's a neat truck, Aunt Lynne. Can we use the upstairs bedroom?"

Lynne didn't know what to say.

She noticed Brad and Abel standing by the door.

Abel shrugged his shoulders. "Gwen and Jed needed help."

"It's no problem. But Eric, I would rather you and Brad use the downstairs bedroom. I even have a TV and VCR in it. I wouldn't want to take the chance of you falling down the stairs or over the loft with your mom about to bring home a new baby."

"I understand. I'll take my bag into the room. Uncle Abel got pizza for supper. He got one pepperoni and one with everything but no fishy stuff. I told him you didn't like the fishy things." He padded off into the back room.

Brad followed. "This is going to be fun, Aunt Lynne."

She noticed that Abel turned to go back outside then entered with two pizzas. He set them on the counter then went back out again. When he entered this time he was carrying a cake along with some red roses in a clear vase. He set them on the counter then closed the front door.

"Happy Birthday, Lynne. I got Gwen to help me order the cake before her water broke. Mabel makes the best cakes. I got you a dozen roses to go with the one Eric and Brad gave you."

Her mouth dropped open. She couldn't believe that he did this for her. "I . . . I don't know what to say. No one has ever . . ." Tears spilled over her eyelids.

"Lynne, don't cry."

"But . . . I'm so happy." The words stammered out. She walked over to him and threw her arms around him.

He returned the hug, holding her close to him. She smelled fresh. He could smell the jasmine again. He lowered his head and her hair breezed against his chin. Gwen was right—he was falling in love with Lynne Murphy. He wanted her to stay in his arms always.

"Aunt Lynne," Eric said, his voice trailing from the bedroom.

She pulled away and tilted her face to Abel's.

"You on the sofa. I'll check on the boys. We need to eat before the pizza gets stone cold."

She quickly wrapped her hands around his neck and pulled his lips down to meet hers. In one sweeping motion she kissed him, then let go. "Thank you, Abel. Thank you."

As she walked over to the sofa and sat down he knew that she was happy because he took time to remember her birthday. The kiss wasn't for the material things that he bought her. Instead it was for being there for her and caring. Yes, Lynne Murphy was a woman that he was easily falling in love with.

Abel peered into the bedroom. "Okay boys, Aunt Lynne is on the sofa. Ready to eat some pizza then go for cake and ice cream?"

Eric rubbed his tummy then licked his lips. "You bet I am. Come on Brad, I'll race you to Aunt Lynne."

Brad took off before Eric even got a chance for his feet to hit the floor. He was on one side of Lynne when Eric and Abel made their entrance.

Eric sat on the other side of Lynne and held her hand. Abel brought the pizzas and sat them on the coffee table then he handed each of them a paper plate.

Together the four of them chatted and ate pizza. Eric and Brad continued to lean on her arm and give her hugs.

"Okay boys, I think Aunt Lynne needs a little breathing space. She's not going to vaporize if you let her go."

"Okay Uncle Abel," Brad said. "Can we play a game when we have our cake and ice cream? I saw the checkers game in the room and we know how to play. Remember, Uncle Abel? You and Aunt Ilene taught us to—" He stopped, then pursed his bottom lip upward. "Sorry Uncle Abel, I didn't mean . . ."

"It's fine. We did teach you boys how to play when you came over. Of course you were so little that you didn't understand how we were playing. We were doing most of the playing for you. Eric was so small. And we had to play give-away a lot."

"But I could be Aunt Lynne's partner and Brad your

partner. Just like when we played with you and Aunt Ilene," Eric commented.

Abel eyed both boys. They were so young when he and Ilene would play the game. He remembered how they sat on their laps and watched the two adults playing. They would smile then clap their hands whenever they jumped their opponents then ended up crowning the other. Little Eric was a baby but he still had fun.

"Tell you what, if Lynne is up to it, I'll get the game out as soon as we have our dessert and clean up the mess. But first you have to take a bath. And you can't stay up too late. Tomorrow is a school day. As long as we don't go over eight-thirty. How's that?"

Eric rocked his feet back and forth, then clapped his hands together. "Yes. And Aunt Lynne and I will win."

"Well, something tells me that Brad and I will win." Abel winked at Brad. "What about you, Brad?"

"We sure are going to try. But we can't keep Aunt Lynne up too long either."

"No we can't. Okay cake, ice cream, then a bath."

Abel lit a few candles, then after Lynne blew them out they sang "Happy Birthday." When the cake and ice cream event was finished, Abel took the boys to take their baths. Then they settled down to play checkers.

They were halfway through the game when Eric asked Lynne her age.

"My age?"

"Yes. How old are you today and what did you wish for?"

Abel answered for her. "Eric, it's not polite to ask

a woman her age. And if Lynne tells you what she wished for then it won't come true."

Eric palmed his hands on his chin then rested his elbows on his knees. "What if I guess, Aunt Lynne?"

Lynne smiled at Abel. "If you guess, do I have to agree that is what I wished for? I might want it to really come true."

"Okay, but I already know what you wished for. You wished for a family with children. You're not married and Uncle Abel isn't married. If the two of you got married you could have a baby like Mommy and Daddy. Then no one would be lonely anymore."

Lynne brushed a strand of hair behind her ear and managed to sound casual. "I think I know of a little boy who is getting tired. We should close this game and finish it on the weekend. How does that sound?"

Brad released a yawn. "Yes. Uncle Abel and I are losing anyway."

"I'll go get the covers turned down. Abel, why don't you spend a few minutes alone with the boys?"

Abel gently touched her hand. "You feel up to it?"

"Yes. Oh, were you able to ask the doctor anything about me?"

"I did. He assured me if you continue to listen to me that you will be up and running very soon."

"Hmmm, if I listen to you, huh?" She looked at the time. "I wonder how Gwen is doing."

"I'm sure Jed will phone us as soon as he knows something."

No sooner had Abel finished his sentence than the phone rang. Eric hurriedly picked it up.

"Hello. Yes. I guess." He handed the phone to Aunt Lynne. "Some man named Franklin."

Lynne eyed the phone as if it were poison. Abel saw her reaction.

"Lynne, you want me to take it?"

She leveled her face to his. "No. It's all right." She took the phone from Eric. "Yes," she spoke into the receiver.

"Didn't want the day to pass without wishing you a happy birthday. See you've got some company," Franklin said.

"I do. It's late."

"Not that late. If you were here I'd show you a good time, Lynne."

"Well, I'm not. Thank you for calling."

"That's it?"

"Franklin, I have guests."

"Lynne, since you've moved away, you sure have been frosty to me. Are you still holding a grudge?"

She inhaled a breath then slowly released it. "I don't hold grudges. I'm just tired. It has been a busy day. You know I'm still trying to get settled in."

"I guess you're right. I'm still waiting for you to invite me down."

"Perhaps after the holidays. Look, I'm watching children tonight and they need to be in bed."

"Sure thing, babe. I'll be seeing you soon."

The phone clicked.

One thing that she didn't want was to see Franklin Goolsby. She placed the phone on the hook then stood with her hands by her side.

"Aunt Lynne, was he a bad man? I didn't like the sound of his voice."

She rubbed Eric's head. "He was just an associate I used to work with who liked to steal ideas, sweetheart. You know, like when someone tries to cheat off your test paper when the teacher says no cheating? Well, that was what he did."

"So he's not your boyfriend?" It was Brad asking.

She shook her head. "No. He might have thought he was. But he wasn't. Let me go get the bed ready."

Eric and Brad folded the game and put it in the box. Eric rubbed his eyes then climbed up in Abel's lap.

"I miss Aunt Ilene, Uncle Abel." He rested his head on Abel's chest.

"I do too." He blanketed his arms around Eric. "I miss her a lot."

Lynne stopped short in the hallway. Abel would never be hers. As long as he missed his loving wife who was buried never to return, she would never have a chance with him. Her birthday wish to be with Abel and have children would never come true. She saw Brad cuddle close to them and rest his head on Abel's knees. At least she was able to get them to be a family once more. Without them noticing, she eased out the front door and sat on the rocker.

Chapter Seven

Lynne inhaled a breath. The air was crisp. The night was full of twinkling stars and a brightly illuminated moon. This was the perfect spot to live. She had her own little cabin, a hideaway from others. All she needed now was a family. Ha, that was never going to happen. And not with Abel Mason.

Samson snuggled up to her. He made a few whimpering sounds.

"You're lucky, Samson. You don't know what humans have to go through. What I wouldn't do to be part of Abel's life. To make him happy. I could do that too." She leaned her head back against the rocker and closed her eyes.

Eric sat upright. "I guess we better go to bed. Are you taking us to school in the morning?"

"I am."

"And Aunt Lynne?"

"Yes."

"I really like Aunt Lynne, Uncle Abel. I wish you were married to her."

"Me too," Brad added.

Eric rubbed Abel's face. He still hadn't bothered to shave today. "Can't you still miss Aunt Ilene and marry Aunt Lynne?"

"Boys, it's a little complicated. When you get older you'll understand."

"I don't want to get older. I want to stay little so things are not comeplicaked."

"Complicated," Brad corrected.

"I said that," Eric stated. Brad and Abel shook their heads and smiled. "When I say my prayers tonight I'm going to ask for you and Aunt Lynne to be a family." He looked about the room. "Where is she?"

"I saw her tiptoe outside when you and Uncle Abel mentioned Aunt Ilene. She looked sad," Brad remarked.

Abel sighed. "Come on boys. Let's tell her that we're going to bed."

The phone rang. Brad grabbed it.

"Hello."

"Brad?"

"Daddy! Is Mommy okay?"

"Yes. You have a baby sister. Is your Uncle Abel or Aunt Lynne nearby?"

"Here's Uncle Abel." Brad handed the phone to Abel.

"Hello."

"Got a little girl, brother. Five pounds six ounces. A tiny one. Got dark hair just like Gwen. And the prettiest blue eyes. Remind me of yours. Named her Ilene Renee. Can you and Lynne come by tomorrow after you drop the boys at school? Gwen can't wait for you to see her. She won't even let me hold the little doll. And that's what she looks like. A perfect little doll. You can't know the feeling to be the proud papa again until you hold a little life in your arms. Tell you, I feel rich. Got my family and brother back."

"Congratulations, Jed. How is Gwen?"

"She's doing great. The delivery wasn't too bad. Before that she had some hard pains but she's a trooper, Abel."

"Lynne and I will be by tomorrow."

"The boys a handful?"

"No. They are well-mannered little boys. We are having a fun time."

"Let me tell them good night."

"Here Brad, your dad wants to say good night. Then give the phone to Eric. I'm going to check on Lynne."

He found Lynne rocking in the chair with hands folded in her lap, Samson near her side. He squatted down beside her.

"It's a pretty night."

"Yes. I see why Samson loves the outside life." She ceased the rocking.

Abel slid his hand inside hers. "That was Jed on the phone. Five pounds, six ounces. He never discussed her length or what time she entered the world. His tongue was just flapping with happiness. You'd think that this was his first child."

She tightened her hands over his, holding it secure. It felt so right. "He's just a proud papa."

"They want us to come over tomorrow after we drop the boys off at school."

"How was Gwen?"

"Doing great."

"I'm glad."

"I think he's going to kiss her," a little voice whispered from the corner of the door.

"Shhh, they'll hear you, Eric," Brad whispered back.

"We best go put the boys in bed." Abel leaned upward and kissed her lips softly then whispered in her ear. "We don't want to disappoint them." He lifted her to her feet and helped her inside. "Okay boys, last one in bed is a rotten potato." Abel sneered playfully.

"A rotten egg," Brad shouted as he raced toward the bedroom followed by Eric.

After the boys were tucked in bed and sleeping soundly, Abel took hold of Lynne's hand and walked with her upstairs.

"I was going to work on the swing but it's getting late. It's been a long day so I think I'll call it a night. When we get back tomorrow, I'll go work on the project."

Lynne slid in the bed and rested her back against the headboard. She patted the edge of the bed. "Want to sit a spell, cowboy?" A smile creased her lips.

He thought for a moment then sat down. "I know you heard what Eric said about Ilene and then my words. Brad said you appeared sad. Look Lynne, there's a part of me that is always going to miss her. I was married to her for five years. I was twenty, she eighteen. There's not a day that goes by that I don't think of her. That's why I had to speak to Gwen today."

"Oh?"

"I told her that I was wrong in my past actions. I was in so much pain when Ilene died that I wanted to shut everyone out. I didn't want to be with family at all."

"Death of a loved one is never easy to accept. But to shut your only family out for all those years . . ."

His eyes linked with hers. "I realize that now. I was hurt, Lynne. Deeply hurt. Ilene was my life, my joy. We shared everything together. It hurt badly not having someone there. My parents gone. Ilene gone."

She tilted her head, then slightly chewed on her lip.

"Okay, what is that look for?" he asked while crossing his arms.

"Your statement about not wanting to be with family then not having someone there. It makes no sense. Jed, Gwen, not to mention the boys. You did have someone there, Abel. You've always had someone there. Jed was there even before Ilene came into the picture. I can understand you not wanting to be with family for a while, but three years is a long time."

He uncrossed his arms and took a breath. "I realize that now more than you know. I was wrong in not reconciling with them. I think about that more than ever now. What if you had never bought this cabin? I probably wouldn't even have been told about the baby."

"I don't know about that. I'm sure Gwen would have gotten word to you somehow. I'm surprised Jed didn't stomp up to your cabin and just pull you back with your family. It's never one-sided in anything, Abel."

"So now you're saying Jed is responsible for me not reconciling?"

"No. I'm only saying things are never one-sided. You may think they are but believe me there are two sides to each story. I do feel that you and he have wasted too many years. I would have loved to have had a family, a brother, a sister . . . I mean a real family besides that of the orphanage."

He lowered his head, glancing at the floor, then faced her.

"I'm having mixed feelings since you've arrived. My heart is a bit confused right now."

"Can I inquire if it's good or bad?"

"Troubled. But it certainly isn't bad. I don't know if I should tell you this now, but I'm feeling . . . what I mean is, you stir something inside me that I haven't felt in a long time."

"I see."

"You are a real special lady, Lynne Murphy."

She stretched her hand to his and gloved it inside hers. "And you are a kind and caring man, Abel Mason."

"When I talked to Gwen today, I allowed part of my heart to open up. Not only about the past but the present as well."

"I'm sure she was a good listener."

"She always has been. I told her when I lost Ilene it was mentally and physically devastating."

She swallowed. "I'm sure it was for you."

"You have made me see things in a different light, Lynne. Thanks to you my heart that was closed for repairs has been partly open."

"I'm glad. I know two boys that are extremely happy."

He released a warm smile that sent tiny sparks over her body.

"You've thought of how it would be to be married to me, haven't you, Lynne?"

The lump was tightening in her throat. "Abel, I've never been in love before."

"Not even with this Franklin?"

Her eyes locked with his. "Never. He wanted more in our relationship. He pushed. I pulled away. His kisses never meant anything. Then I discovered that he was sneaking around looking at my laptop. I always send samples of designs to Mack before I do the final drawings. Franklin got them, saved them on disk, then emailed them to Mack. Said they were his works. But when Mack saw me bring in the final exhibits he knew that the drawings that Franklin had emailed to him weren't his. There were words. Franklin thinks that I'm still mad over a little tiff."

"That's what he calls it?"

"Yes. He was the reason I was flustered the other night when I was running. He had phoned here. Continues to push, asking when I'm going to invite him down. He means nothing to me, Abel. Absolutely nothing. He was demanding, made me feel as if I was inferior to him. Domineering and cold—that's what he is."

"And there was nothing more in the relationship?"

"No. I admit that he confessed his undying love for me but I found that to be nothing but empty words. I had a conference that I had to attend for three days. The day after I left he immediately went out with another woman. The day after he had confessed his love to me, Abel. Empty words and broken promises. That is all that I would have received from Franklin if I had decided to make him a part of my life."

Abel took her hand and brought it to his lips. He bestowed a kiss to it. "I'm sorry he did that to you. Stole your designs as well as part of your heart. I don't think that he needs to be bothering you. He doesn't have your address?"

"No. He got my number through Information."

"He's probably all talk."

"I hope."

"Did you have a happy twenty-first birthday?"

"Are you trying to find out my age, Abel Mason?"

He snapped his finger. "Ah shucks, you found me out."

"Twenty-three, Abel."

"Still a young lady. So did you have a good birthday?"

"Yes, but I didn't get to tell you of my other present today."

"Oh?"

"Mack, my boss, phoned me to wish me a happy day. Seems that he had good news. Anna Lindfors, the famous children's book writer, would like for me to draw her next series of books."

"That's great. I've heard of her."

"But there's one drawback. Seems her publicist doesn't want her to go with me. She wants to go with someone else that is known more than I am. Anna wants me to come up and show her how well I can sketch when she throws the ideas out."

"So what's the problem?"

She shifted her hand from Abel. "Seems she wants me to come up a couple of days before Thanksgiving." She sighed. "If the weather turns too bad for traveling,

I would be stuck there for the holiday. I promised the boys and Gwen."

"Can't you change the day?"

"I asked but that is the only day that Anna can get away. She wants to spend time with her family too."

"Perhaps if you explained further."

"I tried but I don't want to ruin this chance. With this I would have the door open to other projects. You understand?"

"Yeah."

She didn't like the way his *yeah* sounded.

"What does that mean?"

"Nothing." He stood to his feet. "We should turn in and get some rest. I'll camp out on the sofa again."

"Wait. Something is bothering you."

He shook his head. "You were so gung-ho to get me with my family for the holidays and have us both a place set and now you wait until just before the grand event to go on your project."

"My project? Look Abel. I'm a single woman. I don't have a man to look after me or bring home a paycheck for me. What am I supposed to do? What would you do? Just turn down this once-in-a-lifetime deal?"

"You have to make that decision. But you shouldn't make promises to the boys that you can't keep."

She leaned upward in the bed. "*I shouldn't make promises?* Just when did this all turn toward me?"

"You interfered when I strictly asked you not to, to get me back with my family, and now you are the one that is sailing off for the holidays."

Each word that pressed off his tongue was irritating her more by the minute. "I believe you're jealous."

"Jealous?"

"You're the one that wants me here but you won't admit it. You're using the boys."

"And that makes me jealous?"

" 'Cause I have something that might make a name for myself."

"Lynne, you're crazy. Go to sleep. We've got to get the boys to school in the morning." He turned and started down the stairs.

"About what you and Eric said."

His footsteps stopped abruptly. He swirled around and eyed her.

"How you and he missed his Aunt Ilene?"

"I'm not supposed to miss someone that I was married to for five years?" He pounded a hand to his chest. "Someone that I loved the moment I saw her?"

"I didn't imply that. But put yourself in my place. How can I compete with someone who is buried, Abel? You said you have confused feelings. What about me?"

"So that's why you decided to sneak outside."

"Sneak?"

"Brad saw you go outside after Eric said what he did. But you failed to hear the rest."

Surprise covered her face.

"Yes, Lynne. Would you like to hear? Eric said he really liked you. Brad too. They asked me why I wouldn't marry you. Then Eric wondered why I couldn't still miss Aunt Ilene and marry Aunt Lynne. Even said when he said his prayers tonight that he was going to pray that you and I were a family."

"He said that?"

"Does that surprise you? They may be small kids but they are smart."

"Was anything else mentioned?"

"I did tell them that it was a bit complicated. I told them they would understand when they got older."

"Do you even understand now, Abel?"

"How can I when my heart says go one way and then—" He paused, inhaled a troubled breath, then swept his eyes over her. "I told Gwen that I thought I was falling in love with you, Lynne. The credit is due you for bringing me back to my family. You opened that tiny opening in my heart. I can't really explain it now. I doubt if I ever will be able to understand what really happened."

He paused for another breath. "All I know is you helped me see a family was important. When Ilene died and I was thrown into a web of hurt, I turned my back against my family. I can admit that now. At the time I thought it was the right thing to do. You have made me see my mistake. Like I said when I kissed you early this morning . . . Why did you have to come here? You see what you've done to me? To my heart? A beautiful woman fell into my arms and started a feeling inside me that I hadn't felt in a long time. I see your button eyes, smell the jasmine that lingers on your hair, your soft skin. I can't sleep at night, Lynne."

"I wasn't aware."

"How could you be? I never told you. I've seen the way you look at me. The way you speak of me to Jed. The tone in your voice is full of love."

"So where do we go from here?"

"Apparently you've already made that decision."

She tilted her head sideways.

"New York. Your deal with Anna Lindfors."

"I can be a wife and have a family and be an artist, too, Abel."

He looked at her long and hard for a few minutes. What he wouldn't do to take her in his arms right now and kiss her. Marry her and live until death us do part. He shut his eyes and opened them. Until death us do part . . . just like Ilene. But Ilene was gone and Lynne was here. The family loved her. She had brought him back in contact with his family once more. And the boys were wonderful. He never wanted to leave them again.

Lynne watched his expressions but couldn't make them out. "What is the real issue here, Abel? Please tell me. You don't want a wife that works or you can't get Ilene out of your head to really accept the love for another woman? Anyone can say I love you but meaning it from the heart is a different story. You said your heart had been closed for repair and was slowly opening. I am trying to heal that hurt. Let me help you, Abel."

He inhaled a breath. He knew everything she was stressing to him was true so what was the real reason? He closed his eyes then opened them. He didn't wish to discuss anything further tonight. "Good night Lynne. We have to take the boys to school in the morning, remember?"

"But Abel—"

"Good night. If you need anything, call me. I'll come up the stairs." He turned and took the steps in three strides.

Wonderful, he had gotten the last word in. And what was all that about? If he didn't want her to leave to meet Anna Lindfors, all he had to say was don't go. *Stay here with me until after the holidays.* Was his pride so high on a pedestal that he couldn't lower himself to ask?

But it wasn't just the leaving on the holidays, it was having a career and a family at the same time. But she could do both. She was working from the home. She had her own hours.

She breathed another sigh. She didn't care. She fluffed the pillow and laid her head down. She closed her eyes but one thing that she wouldn't get was sleep. He had her mind in a tailspin.

Lynne sat up in the bed. She started to get out and march down those stairs and confront him again. What did he want from her? He had told Gwen that he thought he was falling in love with her and just afraid to admit it? Abel Mason falling in love with her, Lynne Murphy?

Anna Lindfors or Abel Mason? What was she going to do? He wasn't helping. Resting her head on the pillow again, she tried closing her eyes. This was something that she had always wanted. Then again finding a man like Abel was something she had longed for all her life. A lifetime commitment.

She rolled on her side then rolled back to her other side. Sleep was going to be hard to gain tonight and it was all thanks to a man on her sofa who was stirring her heartstrings.

Chapter Eight

"There's our little angel, Momma," Jed said as the nurse entered with the baby. He had a glow on his face brighter than the sun.

Lynne could tell that he was a proud daddy. She caught Abel eyeing Jed and the baby as the nurse handed Ilene to Jed. Gwen's countenance was radiant. She was holding Abel's hand.

This was what Lynne hoped for. A loving husband, children, close-knit family ties. She and Abel had barely spoken while getting the boys ready for school this morning. All they wanted was a bowl of cereal and orange juice then they got their backpacks and headed out to the truck with Samson in tow.

He had climbed in the back with the boys and was looking forward to the trip into town. After the boys were safe inside the school Abel and Lynne headed to see Gwen and Jed. Samson obediently got into the back of the truck and laid down patiently waiting.

"Lynne, I'm sorry you didn't get to spend time with

my midwife. She was on her way to help deliver another baby," Gwen mentioned as she patted Abel's warm hand. "Jed and I discussed the different ways that childbirth was offered to us now days. I had heard about Frances being a midwife. She was great."

"But the doctor was here when you delivered?" Lynne asked.

"Oh yes. He and Frances go back many years. He has no problems with her chipping in to help."

"That's good. I've seen some places where even doctors don't like nurses to throw in their two cents' worth."

"Yes. I've seen that too. So sad isn't it?"

Lynne nodded. Jed was still cooing over the baby. He stood to his feet.

"Here, Abel, you hold Ilene for a while."

Gwen released Abel's hand as Jed placed the tiny infant in his arms.

Lynne edged over to Abel and glanced at the tiny infant with dark hair and pretty blue eyes like Abel's almost. Of course Gwen had a blue shade of color too. "She is an absolute doll." Her finger wrapped around the wee hand. She leveled her face to Abel and smiled who returned the favor.

"Here, you hold her."

"Abel, I couldn't. What if I—"

It was too late. The tiny infant was planted in her arms. Her eyes misted. Gwen noticed it.

"Lynne, what is it?"

"She's so precious and perfect. She has a mother and a father. Not to mention two little brothers that can hardly wait to see her."

"Don't forget a wonderful uncle," Gwen added.

"Yes, can't forget that." Lynne grinned.

"You look good holding a baby, Lynne," Jed remarked.

"Yes she does," Abel agreed. He kissed Lynne on her forehead.

Both Gwen and Jed were surprised. They exchanged a glance then smiled.

"I think that you should give motherhood a try," Gwen mentioned.

"I need to have a husband first." She handed the baby back to Abel. "Your turn."

Ilene started to squirm and raise her little arms. More tears misted in Lynne's eyes.

"I'm sorry," she said, reaching for a tissue. "I get teary-eyed over little babies."

"We need to find you a groom then you could have all the babies you want." Jed grinned.

Lynne turned her back as Abel handed the baby to Gwen.

"I think this has something else to do than with babies. Why don't you tell them, Lynne?" Abel suggested.

She turned back to face the others. "It has to do with babies."

"And not Anna Lindfors?"

"The children's story writer?" Jed inquired.

"Yes. Seems that Lynne has been offered a chance to draw for her next series of books. That is if Anna approves her work."

"That's wonderful," Gwen said.

"It certainly is," Jed seconded.

"She wants Lynne to go to New York just before Thanksgiving."

"Just before the holidays?" It was Gwen asking.

"Yes." It was Abel answering. "After she gets me to get back with my family, promise the boys that she will be attending Thanksgiving with us, she has to go to New York."

Jed and Gwen eyed Abel.

"Abel, she will be back for the holidays." Jed said.

"Really? Thanksgiving, when the airports are crowded, crazy delays, snow. It doesn't matter if you have a ticket, things happen. I don't want to see the sad look on Eric's or Brad's face."

There was something more going on here. Both Gwen and Jed sensed it. Lynne hadn't had a chance to offer any explanation. Abel was doing all the explaining for her.

"I told Abel that this was a great chance for me. It will open doors."

"And what about your family that you want?"

"Abel, I think that Lynne can have a career and a family. A lot of women do," Gwen spoke in her defense. "Besides, she has her office in her home now. What exactly is all this about?"

Abel turned his attention to Lynne, their eyes locking into each other. He raked his hand through his hair. "If Lynne was so sure-fire to get me with my family again, to make me see that family is important, which she did. I would think that she wouldn't want to disappoint the boys."

Jed exchanged a glance with Gwen. This had nothing to do with Abel being with his family. Abel didn't want Lynne to leave. He wanted her there with him for the holidays. He was the one that didn't wish disappointment.

"Maybe Anna Lindfors would allow Lynne to come after the holidays," Jed prompted.

"Seems she wants to see me the Monday before. But I'm sure that after she seems my drawings, that I will be back home Tuesday," Lynne expressed. "I won't disappoint the boys."

"You can't be sure of that, Lynne," Abel said coldly.

Gwen shifted the baby into her other arm. "Hey you two, I think that everything is going to work out for everyone. I do need to ask if the boys could stay a couple more days. My mom is coming down for a week to help out but until she arrives I could use a spare hand."

"They are welcome to stay as long as necessary. They are having fun in the spare room. And they even played checkers with us last night. We each had one as a partner. Abel and I are enjoying every minute with them."

"Yes, Brad always enjoyed that when they were little. Brad would tell us how Abel would sit him on his lap and be his partner. Eric was so young, but . . . well he was so young but Brad remembers those things." Jed didn't continue. He knew how Abel still clung to Ilene.

Lynne rubbed her hands together. "Well, I think it's time that we left and allowed the mother and child to be alone to rest. Abel has some things to do. I'll be back later to pick up the boys when school lets out."

"We really appreciate this," Jed said.

"Like Lynne said, we're enjoying the boys with us." He reached for Lynne's hand. "You ready then?"

"Yes." She glanced at his hand then gloved hers inside his. "See you both later."

"You bet," Jed said.

They watched as Lynne and Abel walked out the door holding hands.

Jed wiped his forehead. "Whew, what was all that about?"

"Your brother is falling in love with Lynne, Jed."

"You think?"

"I know. But something has to punch him in the rear to get him to wake up and smell the coffee."

"Yeah, I guess you're right. It better not wait too long to punch him."

"No Jed, *it* better not."

After they made a quick stop at the post office so Lynne could mail her drawings to Mack, Abel needed to make one stop to see Gene. He wanted to assure him that the project would be done in time to ship within three days. Lynne browsed around at some of the crafts that the man had to offer in his shop. As many times as she had been to the area, she had never even been inside this shop.

"No hurry, Abel," Gene mentioned. "They know you are good for the work. Of course you probably would like the rest of the money for a little Christmas shopping. With Thanksgiving fast approaching, ol' Saint Nick is right around the corner."

"Probably could at that." His eyes floated over to Lynne who was looking at some of the little wooden figures. There was one in particular that she continued to pick up and admire.

Gene spotted her. "So, little lady, you like that one?" She nodded. "A lot of folks come in and want that particular piece."

"I love dogs and horses. Of course I like this bear.

I'll have to keep this in mind. You have these in stock, the person who makes them?"

He cast his eyes over to Abel. "Yes, I can keep these in stock. And if you want a particular style other than these, I can probably persuade the maker to follow your design."

She rested a finger on her chin and thought for a minute. "If I give you a drawing to go by do you think the maker could follow the design?"

"I'm sure the maker would have no problem."

"Good, I'll get it to you."

"I'm ready, Lynne, if you are," Abel said.

"Yes. You have a really nice shop, Gene. Sorry I missed it those times I came to visit."

"Well you're here now and that's all that matters."

She exited the shop followed by Abel. It was a beautiful sunny day and with Abel walking by her side it was the best day in her life.

Abel parked the truck then walked around and helped her out. Samson tumbled out next.

"It was really good seeing Gwen and the baby, especially holding the tiny infant." She didn't want this moment to end. He would go home and work on his project. She would be alone to flip channels.

Abel brushed the toe of his boot against the pavement.

"Yes, babies are a wonder. You did look good holding her. Like it really suited you, Lynne."

"I hope to have some when I marry. I do love children."

"And animals." He smiled.

"Yes, and animals."

Samson watched them, his head dodging back and forth wondering when they were going to move.

"I should let you get busy on your work, Abel. I was thinking that I could prepare a pot of spaghetti for tonight. The boys would like that."

"They do love spaghetti and meatballs. Are you sure you feel up to going to get them?"

"Absolutely. My ankle is all better. Even the scraps on my cheek have vanished. See?"

His hand palmed her cheek. "Yes I see. Didn't I tell you that I would take care of you?"

Her eyebrows knitted together. "You are incorrigible, mister."

"But you like me that way." His hand fell to his side.

She felt her face flush. She did like him that way.

"I suppose I better get busy." He started walking off.

Lynne slowly started walking to the porch. Samson took a few steps then stopped and looked back. He made a whining sound. Abel stopped and turned.

"Samson, I know what you're thinking boy, but I don't know about this."

Samson whined again.

Abel parted his lips then sighed. "She does smell like a field of jasmine. And those eyes. A man could get lost in those eyes. That long auburn hair. And the way she felt in my arms that day. I'll never forget that sensation as long as I live. You know what this means, Samson—I've never had a woman inside that cabin since Ilene died. It's my first step."

Samson turned his head upward to face Abel then barked.

Lynne heard the barking sound and stepped off the porch. She saw the two of them facing downwind at her.

"Is everything all right?"

"Yeah. Samson and I were wondering if you would like to join us?"

"Join you? I thought you wanted your privacy."

"I'm open to change." He extended his hand.

She ran up to meet them. Abel's hand was still reaching. She gladly accepted it and started the climb by his side. He was open to change, he had commented. This was indeed a great day because of Abel Mason.

Chapter Nine

The cabin was similar inside to Lynne's when she first entered. Of course he didn't have an open loft. He had a stairway that led to two bedrooms upstairs and a bath. In the master bedroom there was a Jacuzzi. The washer and dryer unit was also upstairs. The downstairs housed a small kitchen and a bath to the side but the living room had been converted into a large work area. He had all kind of woodcrafts that he was working on.

"You have a nice shop yourself, Abel. You could take your crafts downtown and sell them. I'm sure other tourists who come into town would find these charming." She picked up some of the small figurines. "These even look better than the ones in Gene's store."

Abel pressed a grin on his lips. "Well, I better get busy."

"I'll just sit over here." Lynne took a chair and sat near the window. "Do you have a pencil and paper?"

"Look in the desk drawer in the corner. You should find some."

"Thanks. I thought that I could do some sketches of the wood piece I wanted to present to Gene. I'll probably do more than one. I want to give the boys something that is made by hand and not from some factory. Of course I'll still probably find them some power robot or ranger or whatever boys go for nowadays."

He chuckled.

Lynne opened the drawer and pulled out a pencil and paper. It was after she closed the drawer that she noticed the pictures standing behind some candles on the desk. One was of Abel and Ilene on their wedding day. The other was of them standing in front of the cabin with Samson. It was no mistaking that the two were in love. Ilene was a pretty woman. Long black hair cascading over her shoulders. Her smile was almost real as Lynne eyed the photos.

"I see you found the items."

Lynne jumped. "Sorry. I wasn't aware you were behind me. Ilene was very pretty."

He inhaled a breath. "She was very beautiful. You know you're the first woman that has been in this cabin since she died." His voice wanted to break.

"Do you think it has some meaning to it?"

He sketched a finger down her arm then turned her around to face him. His lips pressed firmly on hers and kissed her, then lightly he broke the kiss while brushing his lips over hers. "Does that answer your question?"

Breathless. That's what she was. Totally, completely breathless. She nodded then walked back to the chair as he ambled over to finish his work.

For a long time she took the pencil and sketched away. Every once in a while her eyes would wander to him. Every time his hands touched the wood it was as if he was putting his whole heart into it. And from where Lynne sat, she knew that each craft that Abel made was done with his heart and with love.

It was intriguing the way he sculptured the wood with his left hand. Her left-handed Abel. Ready, willing, and Abel, her left-handed man who sent shivers down her spine when his lips brushed over hers. That last kiss was filled with longing. A longing to be with someone again, to love, to cherish. She was so deep in thought a few hours later that she hadn't noticed that the saw had stopped its grinding.

He wiped the dust from his clothes. "Lynne, got an idea. Why don't I go clean up and the two of us can go get the boys?" Nothing. He walked over to her. "Lynne?"

"Sorry, did you say something?"

He tapped the tip of her nose. "Someone is in deep thought with their drawings. I think I'll clean up and the two of us will go get the boys."

"Sounds good. Isn't Samson going?"

"Correction—the three of us."

"Okay."

"When we return while the boys do homework you can prepare the spaghetti. I'll finish some more here then we all can share dinner together. Of course I doubt if Eric has any homework in first grade."

She smiled. She liked the sound of that. It was almost like their family. "You'd be surprised. I hear the teachers start even the young ones out with all kinds of sentences with new words each night." She twisted in the chair. "I'll be here waiting."

"If you have those designs finished we even have time to drop them off to Gene before we get the boys."

"Got them right here."

"Good. I'll be down in a bit."

They were sitting around the table enjoying the spaghetti. The boys had finished their homework. And even though Eric had finished his at school, he had pulled out his crayons and two sheets of paper. He said he would draw a picture of his family and then Aunt Lynne could put one on her refrigerator. He presented his finished homework to Abel which did include taking his spelling words and putting them into sentences.

"Lynne, you were right about making those sentences. I would never have imagined a child so young having that homework."

"Told you, Abel—they start them off earlier now."

"Aunt Lynne, this is good spaghetti and meatballs. You made the meatballs tiny like little marshmallows. I like that. You can get more of them in your mouth that way!" Eric said, grinning.

"It is very good, Aunt Lynne," Brad chimed in. "Don't you think so, Uncle Abel?"

"The best I've had in a long time." He sent a smile to Lynne.

"Thank you. It's such a compliment coming from three handsome bachelors."

The phone started ringing.

"Can I get it, Aunt Lynne? It could be Mommy."
She nodded and Eric went to the phone.

"Hello. Yes, she's here but she's eating dinner." He
crinkled his eyebrows. "I guess so." He covered his
small hand over the phone. "Aunt Lynne, it's that hard
man. Do you want to talk to him?"

"Want me to take it, Lynne?" Abel offered.

She grimaced then slowly rose from the table. "No.
I better see what he wants."

Eric handed her the phone. "I don't like him." He
eased back to the table and cupped his hand in Abel's.

"Hello."

"Hey kiddo, what are you doing?"

"I believe Eric informed you that we were having
dinner."

"Cute kid. I really want to see you, Lynne."

"Franklin we didn't have anything to begin with. I
don't want you calling me anymore."

"Are you seeing someone now?"

"I'm seeing two boys who are waiting for me to
join them at the dinner table."

"I apologized ten times over for our tiff. I shouldn't
have gone behind your back and tried to take your
ideas."

"So you admit that you did try to steal my ideas?"

"I said I did. I wanted to be as great as you, Lynne."

"Franklin, I don't want to discuss this any longer.
It's old news. Please—my dinner is getting cold."

"I really thought that we had something between us,
Lynne. We shared dates, dreams. I miss our times together. Don't you miss any of our times together?"

Lynne played with a strand of her hair. Franklin was
in denial. They never really shared anything together.

She never wanted to share a life with him. The only person she wanted to share a lifetime with was sitting at the table waiting for her return.

"Franklin, I believe that my interpretation of our times together is slightly different from yours. I want to think of my career."

"You'll grow old and alone."

"I don't think I'll grow old and lonely. But I will remember your words and give it some thought."

"Well, go finish your meal. I'll talk to you later, Lynne. 'Bye." *Click.*

She placed the phone on the hook then stepped to the table.

"Is everything okay?" Abel asked when she sat down.

"Yes."

"He sure keeps calling you, Aunt Lynne," Eric stated.

"I think now he knows that there is nothing here for him to continue calling me, dear. What about some ice cream and leftover cake?"

Eric clapped his hands together. "Yes, yes."

"I'll get it." Abel took his plate and put it in the sink. He stepped back over to Lynne, tilted her face to meet his then lightly kissed her lips. "That was a scrumptious meal."

"Uncle Abel, if you married Aunt Lynne, that man would stop calling," Brad prompted.

"Yeah, you're probably right. Now who wants the first slice of cake and ice cream?"

Eric hurriedly threw his hand in the air. "Oh, I almost forgot. My drawings. I put them inside my book bag." He climbed off the chair went to his book pack then returned. He snuggled up to Lynne. "I drew this for Mommy and Daddy. See, there's Brad and me. Mommy and Daddy and baby Ilene in Mommy's arms."

"I bet your mom will appreciate that." She hugged him and gave him a kiss. "What do you think, Abel?"

He knelt down and eyed the picture. "I'd be proud to have that picture, buddy."

"I drew you and Aunt Lynne one too. When you come to visit her it will be on her refrigerator." He held it out. "It's you and Aunt Lynne. And Aunt Lynne is holding your baby."

Lynne pressed her lips together.

Abel cast her an eye and winked. "You know, Eric, I think we need to put that on the refrigerator now. There are a couple of magnets. Can you reach them?"

"I sure can." Eric pranced over and pinned the picture on the refrigerator door. "I think it looks pretty. Of course I can't draw as good as you, Aunt Lynne." He eased back to the table and slid on the chair.

"I bet when you get older you will." She smiled.

"Okay sport, eat your cake and ice cream. I've got to go finish the swing I'm working on. I want you and Brad to eat, then take a bath."

"No checkers tonight?" It was Brad asking.

"Not tonight, boys. But we'll have the weekend to finish the game. Lynne, here's your cake and ice cream."

"Thank you."

The phone rang again.

"I'll get it." Eric raced to answer. "Mommy, hi. I miss you and Daddy. Yes, Brad and I are being good. We are always good. We had spaghetti tonight. Aunt

Lynne makes the best spaghetti. Will you get mad at me if I tell you that it tastes better than yours?"

Lynne exchanged a glimpse at Abel then almost choked on the piece of cake in her mouth.

"All right, you can talk to Brad now. I love you and Daddy, and sister Ilene." Eric stretched the phone to Brad. "Mommy wants to talk to you."

Eric sat down at the table while Brad spoke on the phone.

"Mommy wants your recipe, Aunt Lynne. She says she can only buy spaghetti in a can."

"That's true," Abel admitted. "Said she could never prepare it."

"It's all in the spices." She arched a brow at Abel.

"Uncle Abel, Mommy wants to talk to you."

Abel took the phone from Brad. "Yes. We are doing great. You worry about yourself and that little niece of mine. Don't worry about what Eric says. You know how curious kids are. Yes I know. Brad has always been the mature one too. But I am beginning to think that Eric is following in his footsteps." Abel cracked a smile.

"Gwen, he's a small boy. Lynne and I don't think anything about it. We sort of like it."

Lynne turned her head to Abel. Could he read her thoughts?

"Tell my brother to go home and get some rest. Oh, well that is good that they are allowing him to stay with you. Maybe this way the both of you will get some rest without worrying so much about the other. Love you, Gwen. And that goes for the baby and Jed. Yes, I am glad I came to see you that day too. It's a day that I will never forget. You're right, I do owe it all to Lynne. I'll give her your best. I'll try not to. Yes, I will consider the other as well."

Abel hung the phone up and went back to the table. "Gwen sends her love. Jed is staying with her." *By the way, she thinks that I'm falling in love with you. She thinks that I should tell you, Lynne.* The words floated through his mind as he gazed into her beauty.

"I wondered could he do that since they weren't going through the hospital. I think it's kind of warm and homey that children can be brought into the world this way again. I mean having the baby the way you choose."

"People do have a choice, I'm told."

"With it being her third child, I can understand why she doesn't want to have to go to a hospital again. I never really cared for hospitals myself. Of course I only had to go to have my appendix removed. Maybe because I was alone and had no one." She shrugged her shoulders. "Then again I'm partial to the smaller clinics in the rural areas."

He listened to her every word. Her words were always softly spoken when they pressed off her lips. "Well, I guess I better see the boys get their bath before I head out."

She swept her eyes over him. Again they had shared conversation. It made the empty void in her life feel enriched.

While Abel got the boys ready for bed, Lynne hurried and did the dishes. When their baths were done, Abel read them a story then said he would be back in a couple of hours. He wanted them asleep and ready to take on a new day.

After Lynne finished her bath, she slipped on her

pajamas and snuggled on the sofa with a book and the remote. A yawn escaped her lips. She was tired but every time she shut her eyes Abel appeared. She saw the way he handled the boys. How he used his hands to carve the wood. He took such special care of everything he touched. And now with each passing day, he would drop a kiss to her lips or rub a finger down her arm. She wondered why he and Ilene had never had any children after five years of marriage.

"Oh Abel, I love you. I thought that I would never say that but I love you so much."

Brad and Eric tiptoed back and slid under the covers.

"Did you hear that, Brad?" Eric whispered.

"I was beside you in the hallway. Of course I heard it. But Uncle Abel wasn't around."

"She loves Uncle Abel. What are we going to do to get them together?"

"I guess we better keep saying our prayers. But this time pray even harder."

"Maybe you're right," Eric said, pressing his little hands together to pray.

Chapter Ten

When Saturday morning rolled around Lynne was greeted by two pairs of eyes staring directly at her.

"Brad, Eric, is something wrong?" She shifted in the bed, yawning.

"Are you sick, Aunt Lynne?" Eric inquired.

"Sick? No. Why do you ask?"

"You're still in bed," Brad answered.

"Did I oversleep? What time is it?"

"It's already after seven o'clock," Eric informed her.

"Wait a minute. Isn't today Saturday?"

Eric nodded his head up and down. "Yes and you are missing it."

"Missing what? There's no school today. This is the day we get to sleep in, right?"

The boys shook their head no at the same time.

"Brad, I told you that she must be sick to still be in bed."

Lynne sat up leaning halfway on her elbows. Abel

stood at the top of the stairs. His hair was half combed. His blue plaid shirt was halfway out of his jeans and he wore no shoes only his white socks. He looked wonderful to her this early in the morning.

"Honey, I'm not sick."

"But you aren't out of bed," Eric reminded.

"What time is it, again?"

"After seven." Eric pointed to the clock.

"You said I was missing it?"

"Yes, Aunt Lynne. Cartoons. Today is cartoon day. Brad and I finally got Uncle Abel up. We were surprised that you were still asleep. We tiptoed up here to see if you were sick."

"Cartoons?"

"Yep," Abel answered.

"And if you don't hurry and come downstairs, you are going to miss Scooby-Doo," Eric informed with raised eyebrows.

"Scooby-Doo?"

"Yes, the dog and—"

She palmed a hand in the air. "Yes, Eric. I know who the characters are." A yawn escaped from her lips.

"We have breakfast for you and Uncle Abel," Brad said.

"Breakfast?"

Brad nodded. "And if you don't hurry downstairs the milk will turn soggy in your cereal. That is what Daddy always tells us."

Eric reached for her hand. "I'll help you up."

Her eyes shot to Abel's.

"Don't look at me. That is unless you're sick."

"Boys, give me time to wash up and comb my hair and I'll be down."

"All right, but do you want us to wait?" Eric asked. "You might fall back in the bed and go to sleep and miss everything."

"I don't think that will happen. Just give me a few minutes."

"Okay, Aunt Lynne. We will have the breakfast on the coffee table when you come down," Brad said.

Lynne eyed the clock. There went her Saturday morning for sleeping in.

Once her footsteps hit the bottom step Eric grabbed her hand and pulled her to the sofa. "We have a place for you right beside Uncle Abel."

"But I don't have to sit this close. The sofa is roomy."

"Not when Brad and I stretch out beside you. And the chairs are not for sitting when cartoons are on. We all have to sit on the sofa."

"That's a new one for me."

"Me too." Abel grinned. "They told me the same thing."

"This bowl of corn flakes is for you, Aunt Lynne." Brad handed her the bowl. "This one is for you, Uncle Abel. We have juice for each of you on the coffee table."

"Aren't you and Eric eating?" Lynne wondered.

"We had our cereal at six o'clock."

Lynne swallowed. "That early?"

"Oh yes. We didn't want to miss any of the cartoons."

Eric slid near Lynne while Brad climbed next to Eric.

Lynne exchanged a look with Abel then spooned some of the corn flakes in her mouth. Soggy was right. How long had the cereal been sitting in the milk?

"Good, isn't it Lynne?" Abel asked.

She nudged a fisted hand against his thigh.

They finished the cereal then drank the juice. The boys seemed content that they were all together watching cartoons. Abel stood to his feet.

"Where are you going, Uncle Abel?" Brad quizzed.

"I need to put another log on the fire and rinse out the bowls."

"No. I will take the bowls and glasses. You can put a log on the fire then sit back beside Aunt Lynne."

Prisoners. That's what they were. She pasted a grin on her lips and sent it to Abel. For some reason he didn't seem to mind the situation this morning.

An hour passed and Lynne had her head halfway on Abel's chest sleeping. Abel had his head halfway hanging over her. The phone rang and Eric jumped to answer it.

"Hello," he whispered.

"Eric, honey, this is Mommy. Is everything okay?"

"Yes Mommy."

"Why are you whispering?"

"Don't want to wake Uncle Abel and Aunt Lynne."

"Oh, they are sleeping in today?"

"No. Brad and I woke them up to watch cartoons with us. We gave them cereal for breakfast and juice."

"Then why are you still whispering?"

"After they ate, Aunt Lynne fell asleep on Uncle Abel's chest. He is laying his head on her too, but it is sort of sideways, Mommy. Brad and I made sure they sat side by side on the sofa."

"I see."

"Brad and I overheard Aunt Lynne talking to herself the other night. She said she really loved Uncle Abel. I don't know why she just won't tell him. And we don't understand why Uncle Abel just won't marry her."

"Eric, honey, some things grownups have to do on their own."

"Well, some grownups are taking a long time to make up their minds."

Gwen smiled. She could just picture her young son's face as he was expressing himself now. "Can I say good morning to Brad?"

"Yes Mommy. I love you."

"Love you too, honey."

Eric handed the phone to Brad. "Just remember to whisper."

Abel shifted on the sofa a bit as he listened to Eric. He had heard the phone ring but didn't move for fear of waking Lynne. He knew she was exhausted. She put her whole heart and soul in taking care of the boys and spending a lot of time with them. He wanted her to get a little more rest.

He could smell the jasmine that still lingered way over in the morning on her soft flesh. Her hair draped over his chest. This was a cozy moment with her that he felt most welcome. So she had said she loved him. That was nice. Maybe the Franklin character really didn't mean anything to her. Of course he had no reason not to doubt her word the first time. He wondered could he make it work with her? Make a lifetime commitment with her? He needed to let go of the past. Needed to find love again. Ilene wouldn't want him pining away his life the way he was. And ever since Lynne had fallen in his arms that one day, there was a certain sensation that he was feeling for her.

Oh Lynne, do I dare trust myself to tell you how I am feeling about you?

By late afternoon, Gwen phoned to inform Lynne that the boys could come home now. She missed them and her mother had arrived early. Abel helped to gather their items.

"I'll miss you and Uncle Abel," Eric said, "but I am glad to be going home. I have missed my room. Of course I have missed Mommy and Daddy too. And we haven't even seen our baby sister. Mommy wanted to make sure that she was all settled in."

Lynne rubbed his hair. "Yes dear, I know. I'll miss you and Brad."

"But you will come to visit?" It was Brad asking. "And you will have Uncle Abel here with you?"

Abel faced her, his hand gently touching her elbow.

"Yes. But Uncle Abel will be staying in his cabin now."

"He's not that far away," Eric said.

"No, I'm not." Abel knelt down and hugged both boys. "I think we best get you home before your dad comes looking for you. Go on out to the truck, we're right behind you."

Abel waited until the boys had stepped out the door. He cupped his hands on her shoulders then linked his eyes with hers.

"Abel, is something wrong?"

"No. Yes." He casually shook his head. "Now that they are going home, I suddenly feel alone again. Lynne, I don't want to feel alone again. These past few days since I got back with Jed and Gwen have been wonderful." He blanketed his arms around her holding her close to him for a moment. She smelled so nice. His fingers softly fumbled through her hair. Then he stopped and pulled her back to look at her again. "I've enjoyed this time that we have had with the children."

"I have too, Abel." Her hands framed his face. "And each day will continue to be wonderful cause you have your family back. And now you have a beautiful new niece." *And you have me, Abel.* She smiled. How she badly wanted to tell him how she felt. But until he had buried a ghost that he still longed for, she couldn't bring herself to admit her true feelings. He had to let the past go before they could have a future together. It was only fair.

"Lynne, I—" But he didn't finish. His lips softly brushed over hers. The kiss was spine-tingling for both of them. He pulled away and ran a finger over her lips. "We should get the boys to see their parents and new sister."

"Yes Abel, we should."

"Now are you sure that you don't want us to keep the boys any longer?" Lynne asked thirty minutes after they arrived. Gwen's mother had everything in her capable hands. Gwen and Jed were like guests in their own home.

"No. Mother wants to take care of all of us. She's always been this way. Jed loves her to death."

"The absolute greatest mother-in-law," Jed boasted.

"I heard that, Jed," Mrs. Barten mentioned. "It won't win you any points." She laughed.

Lynne liked her the moment she was introduced to her. She was shorter than Gwen was, slightly plump with gray hair. She was the perfect picture of a mother and grandmother who loved her family and enjoyed doing for them.

"Just keep tossing kind words to her, Jed. You know she will bake us another caramel cake if you keep dropping hints." Mr. Barten said. He had decided to join his wife to be with his daughter and family. It had been a welcome surprised.

Lynne marveled how close the family unity was. Gwen's family was a treasure that she hoped to belong to one day.

"Abel, you and your girl going to stay for supper?" Mrs. Barten said taking the baby from Lynne. The boys had wanted her to hold Ilene for a while.

"Yes, Uncle Abel. Why don't you and Aunt Lynne stay for dinner?" It was Eric asking.

"Because we have plans," Abel answered. "I'm taking Lynne out to a nice restaurant."

"Oh wow, just the two of you?" Brad asked.

"Yes, just the two of us. You think Samson could stay out in the garage until we get done with our dinner? Then we will swing by and pick him up."

"Can he, Daddy?" Eric asked.

He and Gwen exchanged a look. Abel taking Lynne out to eat? That was a good sign.

"Yeah. I think we can find something for him to eat tonight."

"Can he stay the night, Uncle Abel?" Brad asked.

Abel rubbed the top of Brad's head. "Sorry sport. I can't part without Samson that long. I need him with me at night. You understand? Samson is all I have left."

"But you have us, and Mommy and Daddy. You even have Aunt Lynne," Brad offered.

"Yes son, I know. But Samson . . . well, he is a part of me that goes back when—" He stopped and looked around.

Brad took hold of his hand. "We know. When you had Aunt Ilene then lost her. I understand, Uncle Abel. He's like your security blanket."

"You could say that."

"Just remember that you have all of us in this room too."

He hugged Brad to his side. "I'll always remember that. But you may have to remind me often." He extended his hand to Lynne. "You ready to go?"

She took his hand and rose to her feet. "Yeah. Mrs. Barten maybe another time. I would love to try your caramel cake. Especially before you have to leave."

"You might as well tell them, honey," Mr. Barten said.

"Mom, you aren't going to bake us a cake?" Jed asked.

"No, son. We thought we would wait a couple of days to surprise you. If it's okay with you, we are staying through the holidays. Dad, here, said his partner could run the shop for a while. He wanted to take some time off."

Gwen stood to her feet. "Oh Mom, Dad, that is wonderful. We were hoping that you could stay through the holidays. Even Jed said it would be wonderful."

"It may be through Christmas." She grinned.

"Even better," Jed said. "Maybe I'll get four of those cakes."

"Jed Mason," Mrs. Barten said with a shake of her head.

They all laughed.

The mother eyed Abel. "And you young man, I expect to see you and your girl at our table come Thanksgiving Day. It's not that far away."

Lynne exchanged a glance with Abel. He gloved his hand in hers tighter. If he had his way, she would be there for sure.

"Lynne and I will be glad to grace the table, Mrs. Barten. We will be back later to get Samson."

"Save room for dessert. I'm making a caramel cake."

"I can hardly wait." Lynne smiled.

Eric and Brad watched as they walked out holding hands.

Eric whispered to Brad. "I think that our prayers are going to come true. Let's go play with Samson."

"What are those boys up to?" Jed asked as they trailed out to the garage.

"They are trying to play matchmaker," Mrs. Barten said. "I think it's sweet."

"I do too, Mom," Gwen agreed.

Lynne started to go inside the door then stopped. "Abel, you didn't tell me where you were taking me. I don't know what to wear."

"Just wear whatever you are comfortable in. I thought we would go to the Embers. I've reserved a table by the fireplace for us. It's casual attire. I'm going to change. Probably slip on a pair of dress slacks."

He glanced at his watch. "See you in about thirty minutes. Is that enough time for you?"

"Yes, more than enough."

Lynne looked through her closet. It was nippy outside and when the sun set, it would be much cooler. Perhaps she should wear her navy suit. Mack always said she looked professional and quite stunning when she wore it into work. It would be warmer too, as it clung to her body. She decided for it.

Abel was knocking at the door as she slipped on her navy pumps and adjusted the collar to the blazer. She opened the door and was taken back. He stood gazing at her in black dress slacks, a blue shirt, with a black jacket. The blue shirt really complimented his eyes.

"Abel, you . . . look great."

He swept his eyes over her. He had yet to see her in any dress or suit. She was beautiful.

"I have to admit you are a knockout, Lynne." Her auburn hair cascaded off her shoulders. He remembered how he had allowed his fingers to fumble through it earlier today. "You ready, beautiful?" He extended his hand.

A smile enveloped her lips. "Yes Abel, I am more than ready."

Abel was able to get a table close to the fireplace. There was a roaring fire going when they took their seats. A smile crossed Lynne's face. It was as if Abel told the restaurant to have this setting just for her. The ambience of the whole room was delightful. Even the candles burning on the table seemed to dance every time she released a smile. Abel allowed his eyes to travel over the menu and watch how she continued to smile. She was so beautiful. Tonight she appeared at her best.

They each gave the waitress their order.

"You like broiled salmon?" he asked as he leaned back in the chair.

"It was a toss-up between it and the steak. I do love steak but whenever I have the opportunity to dine out, I have always loved to order the fish." She smiled. For some reason she didn't wish to talk about the menu. She would much rather talk about the way he looked tonight. The way his hair draped slightly over his fore-head. One little piece that always fell over toward his eyes and she wanted to reach and brush it away just like the first day she saw him.

"I myself am a steak man. Have always loved them medium rare." *Abel, what is wrong with you? Here a breathtaking woman sits across from you and you discuss the menu? Look at her. The way her eyes twinkle. Her jasmine smell tonight sent a tingling sensation through you when she got inside the truck.*

"Abel . . ." She lightly reached over and laced her fingers through his. "I wanted to tell you—"

"Look, our food is here."

She quickly moved her hand away as the waitress set their plates on the table.

Abel took a bite of the steak. "This is good. How's your fish?"

Lynne took a bite. "Good." Didn't he feel the siz-zling agitation that ran through her body when her hand laced through his? Didn't he feel any sparks drifting through the air? How could anyone not feel the sensation breezing through the room?

"You were going to say something before they brought our food." He sent a smile her way that left her spinning.

"I was going to thank you for everything."

It was his time to reach over and grasp her hand. "You have already done that dear lady."

Oh, the way he pronounced dear lady sent a blazing wildfire all through her. His voice was like slow moving molasses. She had noticed that from day one.

He pushed his plate away. "That was delicious. Not as good as the night you cooked me my first steak." He winked.

She thought of that night. There were so many memories that she wanted to treasure always.

"Would you care for some dessert?"

"I couldn't eat another bite." *Perhaps we could share a night of holding hands and just taking a little walk. That would be a sweet dessert.*

He looked at the time. "I suppose we should get the check and head for home."

"Yes. It is getting a little late." She didn't want this night to end.

Abel twirled his thumbs. Why couldn't he let go of the past? Why couldn't he reach out and just touch her? Run a finger down her cheek. Her soft check that he had touched many times. He thought of the times he had come to her rescue. The times they had shared evenings together. *Lynne . . .*

After Abel paid the bill and they walked outside he took hold of her hand. The evening had truly been a delight. The atmosphere warm and cozy by the fireplace with candles lit on the table. He never thought she looked more beautiful and she was swimming in tingling sensations every time her eyes focused on him. It was the perfect moment to express to him her true feelings. She considered it twice then stopped.

He has to be free of any attachment, Lynne, or you won't be his totally. Remember that. He's only now beginning to get closer to you. At least that's a start.

She was so much into her thoughts that she didn't realize they were standing near the truck.

Abel's hands cupped the back of her neck. "Lynne, I really enjoyed this night more than you will ever know."

His eyes linked with hers and she was sure that he was going to reach down and kiss her. She could feel his lips touch hers. The warm heat was already sending electric sparks to her toes. She started to close her eyes waiting for his lips to near her.

"Let me help you in the truck."

That was it. Let me help you in the truck. No kiss. Just cup the back of her neck. Allow a current flow of heat to spoon through her body like fallen snow suddenly melting on a hot summer's day.

She took his hand as he lifted her inside the truck. All she could think about was missing an incredible kiss from those lips.

Not a word was said when they left the parking lot. Abel continued to allow the events of the night to flow through his mind. Why hadn't he kissed Lynne? A missed opportunity. He wondered what she thought of that? A smile spread over his lips. The night wasn't over yet.

Mrs. Barten gave Lynne a huge slice of caramel cake plus another one to take with her. They all had shared conversation over the dessert and Jed noticed how Abel couldn't take his eyes off of Lynne the whole night. They made a striking couple.

That had been an hour ago. Now they sat inside the truck parked outside her cabin.

Lynne halfway played with the bowl in her hand.

"Mrs. Barten makes a killer dessert."

"Yes, Abel. She must be trying to fatten me up."

He rested his arm across the seat then allowed his hand to cup her shoulder. "She's just showing you that you are part of the family."

"I feel like part of the family." She sighed.

"What's wrong?"

"It's going to be different being in that house with no children tonight. I'll never forget their little faces this morning when they thought I was ill because I wasn't up watching cartoons."

Abel chuckled. "They can come up with some things." His finger rubbed the corner of her shoulder. "Ilene couldn't have children. We tried. We went to a doctor to see what was wrong. The doctor said it would take time. Told her not to give up hope. She kept saying she couldn't have any. I knew there had to be a reason. I mean there's a reason for everything. Right?"

She nodded.

"I've heard of some people going sixteen years before having their first baby. I encouraged her not to give up hope."

Lynne leaned her head back toward his arm. He circled it around her until it touched her other shoulder. It didn't matter that the truck was off, that the heater wasn't on. She felt warmth being this near to him. Samson perched on the back seat listening to each word.

"It took Gwen three years until she had Brad. You know how some women are? They get discouraged. Gwen tried talking to her. I think talking to a woman helped her." Abel exhaled a small breath. Once again she felt great near him. The moment felt right. Eric and Brad said she loved him. They had overheard her talking to herself. Most likely eavesdropping knowing those two.

Samson yelped a loud yawn.

"I suppose I better get inside," Lynne said, sitting up in the seat.

"Yes. It is cold out here. I shouldn't have turned off the heat. Listen to me, you would think it's my truck. You offer me the keys as if—"

She tapped his hand. "As if I trust you to chaperone me around, Abel. I told you that the first day you caught me in your arms. I never would loan my truck out to just any man."

He kissed her cheek then swung out of the truck and walked over to help her out. She climbed down as he swung her into his arms. Samson jumped out then he closed the door.

"You are as light as a feather."

"Not if I keep eating this caramel cake. She should start her own bakery here."

Abel stopped at the front door still holding her in his arms as she pulled out the key. He inserted it, turned on the light and stood her to her feet.

"We should open up a family shop. My carving and making of wood. Your drawing and sketching. Mrs. Barten's cakes. Now that would be a nice shop."

This time she ran a finger through his hair and down his cheek. "I believe that would be a great shop."

He pulled her close and pressed his lips over hers. Why couldn't he tell her he loved her? Why? The kiss was filled with longing.

She smacked her lips together a moment later. Had that been a flow of current or what? "Wow. I suppose we should say good night." She didn't want to.

"Yeah. Do you think I could use the truck tomorrow after church to take the finished project to Gene?"

She tapped his chest. "Do you need to even ask?"

"No, guess not." He kissed the tip of her nose. "You get some sleep, little lady."

"I'll try."

As she closed the door and locked it, she could hear him whistling as Samson howled in low key in the background.

Lynne hummed all the way upstairs and even after she had her nightgown on. It was a date. A date with a most handsome man that was spinning her heart. She had wanted him to kiss her after the dinner but he didn't. But that no longer matter. He sure made up for it when he brought her home. That was a kiss she would not soon forget.

She slid under the covers but sleep never came. The cabin was too quiet. There was no Abel on the sofa. His scent still hung in the air. Twice she hit the pillows and turned over in the bed. Finally she crept down the stairs and threw herself on the sofa. Yes his woodsy scent was still there. She clung to the pillow.

"Abel, please let go of the past. You did open up

to me and talk of Ilene tonight. That is a good sign. I'm not trying to take her place. I only want to share your future. I love you, Abel Mason. I really love you." She closed her eyes and sought sleep.

Abel threw the covers off then wrapped the quilt around him. He couldn't sleep. He had been sharing a cabin with a family the past few days. Now he was alone. Back in a house with no one. There was Samson but it wasn't the same. Lynne's fragrance still lingered over him. Her skin was so soft. She was so delicate, so petite. *Face it, Abel, you're in love with that girl. Go to her and tell her.*

He thought about the evening. He had wanted to tell her more. Had wanted to hold her and kiss her senseless. There had been tiny sparks of electricity shooting through his body every time he looked at her during the night.

He stopped by the desk and eyed the pictures then picked one up. "Ilene—tell me what to do. I don't want to betray you. I know you are never coming back. Death never allows anyone to return. I don't know what to do. If it were me, I would want you to go on with your life. Not just sit around with no one to share time with. I wish you could tell me what path to take."

He set the photo back on the desk and walked outside. With the quilt tightly wrapped around him, he slumped in the rocker. Samson whimpered.

"No. I can't sleep. All right, you win. I can't get her out of my mind, Samson. She's under my skin. I love her but I guess I've got too much pride to tell her. I just can't let go, Samson. I'm afraid to get close to a person again. Help me. I need someone to help me."

Samson snuggled next to Abel's feet. With a heavy heart, Abel shut his eyes and tried to sleep. It was going to be a long night.

Chapter Eleven

They had picked up the boys for Sunday school and church, while Mr. and Mrs. Barten drove their car. Jed insisted on staying home to care for Gwen in her recovery. For Lynne it was another fun-filled day with the boys and Abel. She didn't mind at all. After services were over, Eric suggested the four of them go out for a kid's meal. Abel shrugged his shoulders, Lynne agreed, and they set out for four kids' meals.

After sharing a meal and dropping off the boys, they headed to the cabin.

"Lynne, I shouldn't be long. Maybe afterward you and I could go driving out to the Smoky Mountain Park and have a picnic. It will be cool so wear a coat. Ever had a picnic in cold weather?"

"No. But I'm up to new things."

"Good. I'll go get the items loaded, go take them to Gene and be back to get you. Can Samson stay here?"

"I wouldn't have it any other way."

He breezed a kiss over her lips. "I will see you later, pretty lady."

She licked her lips. Oh yes he would. She stumbled into the cabin and raced up to the bedroom to change clothes. Things were really beginning to look up for her and Abel. Maybe he was ready to let go of the past. Maybe he was ready to fall in love with her. She knew she was already in love with him.

Abel had the swing loaded when the phone started ringing. He rushed in the cabin.

"Hello."

"I was trying to reach Lynne Murphy and she didn't answer. She gave me this number. I'm her boss, Mack."

"This is Abel."

"Yes, Lynne has spoken highly of you. All good things."

"We only got back from worship services a few minutes ago. If she was inside the house she should have heard the phone."

"Oh wait. It was my mistake. I don't know what I was thinking. Your number is on the same paper as hers. I accidentally dialed the wrong number. I'm so sorry about that Abel. She gave me this other number in the event she was with you."

"Should I go tell her to call you?"

"No. I need to talk to her about something that has come up. I need to give her the information about her flight the Monday before Thanksgiving as well."

"Oh that."

Mack caught the huge disappointment in his voice. "It's a huge opportunity for her, Abel."

"So is spending her first time with a real family who

has adopted her into their life. Something of which she has never had."

Mack was silent. He let a minute pass before speaking up. "You got a minute or two to chat, Abel."

"It depends. Will I like it?"

"I'm willing to bet you do."

Thirty minutes later Lynne was dressed in blue jeans, a light blue pullover sweater, and her boots. At first she thought tennis shoes then decided the boots would keep her warmer. As soon as she got them on, the phone rang.

"Oh hi, Mack. How are you?"

"Good. You sound out of breath. Were you busy?"

"Just pulling my boots on. What's up? And how is Denise? You haven't told me anymore about the conference in Atlanta."

"That is why I am calling."

"Oh, you aren't coming down?"

"You sound disappointed."

"I am. I was so looking forward to seeing you."

"I was going to go but the doctor wouldn't allow Denise to travel yet. He wants to make sure her foot is completely okay since the surgery."

"I can understand that. I know how you wanted to go to the conference."

There was a pause.

"Mack?"

"Someone else is attending for me."

"Oh?"

"Lynne, I don't know how to tell you, but Franklin is going to the conference for me. He knew I was bringing you the artwork. He said he would take it to you. He isn't going to cause any trouble. He promised. Even said if he did, I could fire him on the spot."

She lightly swallowed. "So he is coming by here?"

"Lynne, I—"

"It's not your fault. I am sure he isn't coming to cause trouble."

"I have to admit that he really has changed since you left. He is a different person around here. I mean he is still Franklin but he has grown up so to speak."

"I really am not looking forward to seeing him again but I feel he really won't cause any trouble." But those were only words; with Franklin he always had a double side.

"Well, I wanted to tell you that he should be arriving some time today. The last time he phoned me on the cell phone he wasn't too far away. I tried calling you earlier but every time I went to place a call, that stupid intercom kept ringing in my office for me. Deadlines and all that."

"You don't have to remind me, Mack. I know how busy you stay. Give Denise my love."

"I will. Oh, before I forget, your information on your flight, Abel has it. I accidentally dialed his number before I phoned you. He said he would give you the information. I also sent you an email too."

"Was Abel okay with everything?"

"Oh yes. He is a very nice man. I can see why you like him. We had a great conversation."

"About?"

"Sorry Lynne, intercom going off."

"No wait a minute. This isn't fair."

"Hmmm, sounds like a familiar tune. Remember

our conversation on your birthday and you wouldn't tell me about that kiss? 'Bye Lynne."

"Mack."

It was too late. The conversation had ended. Lynne shook her head then placed the phone on the hook. Mack was a card. But the thought of Franklin coming by to see her was something that she wasn't looking forward to.

Lynne was about to pour a glass of water when she heard Samson snarling outside the front door.

"Samson, what is it?" She asked opening the door.

A tan rental car was parked out front and a man was getting out of the driver's side. She walked out on the porch.

"It's okay, Samson. It's okay." She walked over and met her visitor halfway. "Franklin." She watched each step he made. He wore a pair of black slacks and a gray pullover. As always his black hair was neatly combed and his face was clean-shaven. Every time she was in his presence he was perfectly groomed and not a crease in his clothes. She often wondered did he ever let his hair down just to have fun. He carried a small box in his hands.

His tall structure bore down over her. A smile gleamed on his face. "Now is that any way to treat your once beau?"

She halfway frowned. "Franklin you were never really my beau."

Samson sneered again.

"That your dog?" he said, cocking his head toward the dog. "Got you a powerful good watch dog."

She crossed her arms. "Here, let me take the box."

"I can sit it inside for you."

"Just sit it on the front porch."

"Not going to show me around inside?" he asked as he placed the box on the rocker then stepped back toward the car.

"I'd rather not. I believe you have a conference to get to. Mack called me and told me you took his place. I do not want any trouble."

"And I don't plan to cause any. I wanted to see you. Make sure you were doing well. Can we go inside and talk?"

"I don't think that's a good idea."

"I'm not after your drawings, Lynne. I only want to try to salvage what we had."

"Franklin, we had nothing. Zip. I tried to tell you that so many times. You and I were only associates. There were no sparks when we kissed. Nothing. I don't mean to sound cruel or spiteful. I don't want to hurt your feelings. You and I just weren't meant to be. There is some girl out there for you, it just isn't me." *Maybe the girl you so eagerly phoned that night I was away.*

He touched her cheek. Samson barked.

"Samson, please. It's all right."

"Man, that dog is protective of you."

"Perhaps you should keep your hands to yourself."

Franklin rested his hands by his sides. "So there is nothing here for me?"

"No, Franklin. Nothing."

"Have you found someone?"

"I think I have."

"He's a lucky man, Lynne. I think that's why I came all this way. I had to see for myself."

"And?"

"The eyes can't always see what's inside another person's heart. I've seen it now. So I'll leave you to your cabin in the woods. And I wish you the best." He turned his head and gave the area a quick glance. "I wanted to come for another reason too. And not to hurt you. The girl I saw after you left . . . well, I have been seeing her. I felt bad because in my own way I felt as if I had been leading you on. I thought I wanted you always in my life. What I mean is—"

"Franklin, it's all right. You aren't breaking my heart. I am not going to cry over this. Sometimes what we think we want is not always what our heart wants us to have. I am really happy for you."

"I do apologize seventy times over again for my actions. I don't know if you understand this but I think that I have matured since you left."

She knew that his words were true. She could tell by his words today. "You were a good friend, Franklin, in your own way. I can see a difference in you. I wish you happiness."

He smiled. "Thank you. I do know one thing. You are a hard act to follow. I'll never forget you. 'Bye, Lynne Murphy. I do wish you the best in all your endeavors."

"And I do you the same."

Without thinking Franklin's hand eased up and cupped her face. Samson acted on impulse. In one huge mad jump, he leaped into Franklin, knocking him down. He was fighting him off with his fists. Lynne was trying to help. In the madcap of it all a hard-balled fist struck her in her left eye hard. She landed backwards. Samson started chewing at Franklin's sweater.

"Samson, stop it!" Lynne squealed. She managed to finally pull him off and hold him but Samson was struggling to get free of her as Franklin hurried to his feet. "Just get in the car and go, Franklin! I guess he is very protective of me!"

"Too protective! At least he only took a chunk out of my sweater and not me." He limped over and got into the driver's side and started the car. Lynne still clung to Samson but he was a handful. By the time Franklin had the car turned around and started to drive down the path, Samson broke free and chased after him.

"Samson, no!" Lynne jumped to her feet. The sound of the squealing tires stopped.

Franklin got out of the car and bent over as Lynne was approaching. "I never meant . . . Lynne, he came running. I didn't know. I've never hurt an animal before." He felt for some kind of heartbeat.

"He's still breathing. Can we get him to a vet?"

Lynne saw the agonizing pain in Samson's eyes. "Yes—we better hurry."

Another vehicle was coming up the path. Her truck. Abel was returning. Franklin saw the trepidation in her eyes.

"Lynne—what?"

"Franklin, you should leave now. Abel is on his way. It's his dog. Please go now. Please."

"Lynne, it was an accident."

"I know, but Abel . . . please, Franklin."

Abel parked the truck and jumped out. He raced over and knelt by Samson. His eyes met with Franklin and saw the torn fabric of his clothes, the appearance of Lynne, and the red forming around her eye.

"It was an accident." Lynne struggled to speak. "Franklin was leaving. Samson darted out in front of the car like . . ." She couldn't face Abel. His eyes were so intimidating.

"Honest man, it was an accident. He attacked me. I tried to get in my car. He spun after me."

"He's still breathing, Abel. We need to get him to the vet," Lynne offered as she gently touched Samson's paw.

Abel quietly dismissed her hand, setting it away from Samson. Her heart lumped in her throat.

"Abel . . ." Her word alone bore sorrow.

He gently picked Samson up in his arms and started walking down the path.

"What is he doing?" Franklin asked.

"Going to the vet. Just leave, Franklin. Leave."

Franklin slung himself in the car and drove away. Lynne walked over to the truck. The keys were still inside. She didn't even bother going inside for her purse. She headed the truck down the path and slowed it near Abel.

"Please get in. We need to get him to the vet. You want him to live, don't you? He could be badly bruised inside. Please Abel. The walk is too long. He needs treatment now."

Abel came to a stop. He hugged Samson to his neck and heard a whimper. He didn't even turn his eyes to Lynne. Instead he walked around to the passenger side where she had the door open. He lifted Samson inside then climbed in. Lynne started to touch Samson's paw but moved her hand quickly away. Abel shot her an icy look then turned his face from her.

* * *

Lynne paced the waiting room. It had been over an hour since Abel had taken Samson in the back room. There had only been two people there waiting when they arrived but as soon as they got their rabies shot, they were gone. She framed her hands over her face. Abel had not spoken one word to her but she had seen tears in his eyes. It was an accident. Why couldn't he believe her? She wanted to call Jed. Abel needed someone here now. What could she do?

The receptionist started to close down her computer.

"Mrs. Hunt, can I please go see how Samson is?"

"Honey, I'm sure Abel will come out and tell you soon. You should go have that eye looked at. Someone really gave you a shiner."

The door cracked open and Abel walked over to her. She was too scared to ask. "Is Samson . . ."

"The doctor said that if he makes it through the surgery he should be all right. Bruised inside. A few tiny cracked bones inside. He's checking for internal bleeding. His right paw wasn't broken but he's not going to be able to use it much for a while."

"But he'll be—"

"I don't know yet, Lynne. I can't bear to lose Samson. If something happens to him, I will have no one."

Heat burned inside her. "No one. What about Jed, Gwen, and the children?"

He grabbed her by the elbow and pulled her away from the desk. "You don't understand. Samson is all that I have left from Ilene. If he dies, I have *no one*. Do I make myself clear?"

Her bottom lip trembled. There it was, all in a nutshell. Ilene, Samson. No one. He wasn't ever going to let go of the past. Anything she had felt for him was all a fantasy. No hope at all for the both of them.

"Lynne?" But his word fell to deaf ears.

The doctor came out and walked over to them. "Young lady, you need to see a doctor about that eye."

"I'm fine, Doc." She willed herself not to shed one single tear. She wouldn't allow Abel to see how hurt she was.

"I came out here to tell you that the next hour will tell us if he is going to make it."

"Can I see him?"

"No!" Abel instantly answered.

"What would it hurt, Abel? He has the will to live but he's missing something. At least let her go back there and tell him she's all right. Maybe Samson wants to know she is okay. Know that she isn't harmed."

Reluctantly Abel permitted it.

Lynne stepped inside the room. She casually picked up Samson's paw. Liquid misted in her eyes. "Hey Samson, everything is fine. You have to get well so we can have lots more fun together. That man, Franklin, he meant no harm. He only came to see if I was happy. You heard me. I told him that I was extremely happy. He wasn't a bad man when he touched my cheek. And the only reason his fist hit me in the eye was 'cause I was trying to pull you off him. He kept saying you were my protector. Now you wake up and get well so you can be my protector once more. You hear me?" Her words cracked.

There was a slight whimper as Samson tried to open his eyes.

"Okay, you've seen him. You've said your peace. Now go." No sooner had Abel uttered the words he was wishing that he could take them back. The hurt look on her face was one that he would never forget. "Lynne, I—"

"You're right, Mr. Mason. I've seen him. You know, I've never called anyone a fool so I won't begin. But you have a family out there and if you are too stubborn to believe you can't go on living and you have no one if something happens to this precious animal then it will be your fault. You probably don't want to hear this but you have taught me more about love since I've been here than anyone else in my lifetime has." She turned and walked toward the door then stopped.

"I realize that you lost someone dear when you lost Ilene but at least you had her for the years you did. I lived in an orphanage, Abel. Gwen, Jed, and the boys are like blood family to me. You came along and gave me a chance to feel a love that I had never known. You made me feel special. I do hope nothing happens to Samson because if you barricade yourself in that cabin over the loss of a loved one again then you deserve what life issues to you."

She shook her head and lightly grinned. "Funny how you have so much to offer people and you just shut them out." She cast him one last look before leaving the room, lightly closing the door behind her. She was determined to get the last word this time. And this time that was exactly what had happened.

Lynne pulled out a couple of the tissues on the table. She felt the keys inside her pocket.

"Mrs. Hunt, please give these to Mr. Mason. Tell him if Samson makes it and can go home—because believe me, he won't allow Samson to stay here tonight. Anyway, explain to him the truck is for him to carry Samson home."

"But how will you—?"

"Can I use your phone?"

"Yes, just hit 9 for an outside line."

He answered it on the second ring.

"Hey can you come over to the vet's office and pick me up? I'll explain when you get here. Thanks. I'll be outside waiting."

Lynne finished the cup of hot cocoa then sat the cup on the coffee table. "Jed, I need to ask you one more thing. Can you drive me home?" She wiped another tear from her eye and waited for his response. She had shed a boat full of tears when he arrived to pick her up. Then had shed more buckets when she got to his house. Gwen's mother had made her some hot cocoa while she explained everything that had happened.

She had started from the beginning explaining when Franklin showed up at the cabin to the scene at the vet. The words had been hard to issue but it was something that had to be released.

"I would suggest you get that eye checked first."

"No Jed. I have some first aid cream. It's all right. I'm worried about Samson now . . . and Abel. Of course it's really over between us now. If you could have heard his voice, seen the cold look in his eyes. Then the way he pushed my hand away from Samson." More tears flowed down her cheeks.

"Listen to me. Over between us. How can it be over between us when we were only friends?" She leaned over and allowed more tears to run out. Sitting back up, she took the back of her hand and wiped her face. "Sorry. I've got to stop this. You know I was in a rush that I didn't even lock my cabin door. I don't even have my license with me."

Gwen gloved Lynne's hand. "I'm sure that Abel will come around when Samson pulls out of it. I know what you told us he said but he's upset now."

"With every right too. I didn't know Samson was going to be that protective of me. He had never done it before."

"I guess he smelled a rat when Franklin came to see you. He probably didn't want the man to come between you and Abel."

"I guess you're right. But all I want to do is go home, take a bath, and go to bed." Her eyes met with Gwen. "Really, there is nothing between Abel and me. I suppose he wanted to pamper me in some way cause I didn't have a family. Or perhaps he thought I was a helpless woman that needed help. As for Samson, Abel told him to guard the place. He was only obeying his master's command."

Mrs. Barten walked to her side. "You should put a compress on that eye as soon as you get home. Why don't you crash here? I'd love to take care of you."

Lynne halfway smiled. "No. But thank you. I really want to be alone."

"I can understand dear. I'll prepare you a care package to take along with you. It might cheer you up later. Of course until that Abel comes to his senses, I doubt the package will really be beneficial." She ambled off to the kitchen.

Lynne let go of Gwen's hand and buried her face

in both her hands. There would never be an Abel in her life. Ever.

Abel couldn't believe that Lynne had left the keys to her truck with him. Was she crazy or what? Samson couldn't be moved tonight so the doctor said he had to stay in the clinic. He was right next door. He would even bunk down for the night in the clinic to keep an eye on him. If he slept well through the night he would be himself in no time. He urged Abel to go home, clear his mind and get some sleep. There was nothing more that could be done now. And if he cared anything for Lynne, he needed to see she had that eye checked. Abel nodded. Lynne's eye had looked blackened the last time he saw her. He was more concerned about Samson to even show any feelings for her. He never should have acted like a jerk with her.

Mrs. Hunt had no clue where Lynne had gone, she expressed to Abel. All she knew was she phoned someone then she was gone. Abel pondered on it for a moment. Of course. Jed and Gwen. He climbed in the truck and headed over there.

"Yes, she was here," Mrs. Banter said when Abel got comfortable on the sofa. "Poor girl had a banged-up face, wouldn't go to the doctor. Was crying her little eyes out over you, Abel Mason." She pointed a finger his way. "You ought to be ashamed of yourself. That girl is in love with you and you have lost her because of your foolish pride."

"Mother, Abel didn't come over to get a lecture," Gwen said. "Would you go see about Ilene? Abel is upset right now."

"No more than Lynne was." Mrs. Banter shook her

head then pointed her finger once more. Her mouth started to open then stopped. She turned and walked away.

"Abel, you will have to excuse mother. She does speak her peace. You know that."

He sighed. "Yes that is something I know."

"And this time I agree with her. You were wrong Abel. Very wrong."

Abel cast his eyes toward Gwen before they rested on her. She had never used that tone with him. He could tell her voice was filled with strong concern for him. Not one of hatred but concern and care. "Do you think Jed will return soon?"

"He was going to take Lynne home and come right back."

Abel paced the room. If he could reverse the night he would. He should never have been so harsh with Lynne. He walked toward the fireplace and leaned near the mantle. He would wait all night if he had to for Jed's return. He had to find out about Lynne.

"I checked everywhere, Lynne, didn't see anyone in here. You sure you don't want to come back and spend the night with us?"

"No. I'll be fine. As soon as my head hits that pillow, I'll probably be out. I hardly slept last night thinking of your brother but that isn't going to linger in my mind tonight."

He cupped her shoulders. "Give it a few days. He'll come back around."

"No. You didn't see the snake eyes or hear the venom in his voice. Whatever we might have had, is over where Abel is concerned. It's really over."

He lightly feathered a kiss to her forehead. "My brother is a—"

"Don't say it, Jed. Please."

"All right. But you promise me if you need us, you be sure to call. We're only down in the valley."

"I will. And pray that Samson will be okay."

"Yes. We all want that."

Jed gave her a hug then left.

Lynne swept her eyes around the room. Whatever she was feeling for Abel was still there. How could she make it go away? "But he doesn't want you Lynne. Didn't you hear his words tonight? He can't bury the past. And you can't compete with a ghost."

She eyed the box that Franklin had brought to her. Jed had been kind enough to sit it inside for her. She thought of Franklin's brief visit. She folded her hands over her face then released them. Time to stop worrying over Abel. She needed to concentrate on her work. She headed for the stairs. After all these weeks how could her heart feel so much for a man that she really didn't know much about? He had a brother with a family. He was a widower. He enjoyed his privacy. He did wonders with wood when he was carving and making swings and benches.

She stopped at the top of the stairs and looked down over the loft. None of those things mattered. The only thing that mattered was that she loved Abel Mason. He was tall and lean with arms that wrapped around her and kept her safe. Blue eyes that penetrated all the way to her soul. The night he took her out to dinner he had lumbered lovingly over her like a strong oak sheltering her with its branches. He made her feel safe. Feel warm inside.

She palmed her hands over her ears to stop the silent sounds. *Stop it. Please stop it. He doesn't care for me. And if something happens to Samson . . .* She shook her head. She couldn't think beyond that. Whatever she wanted to have with Abel was never going to happen in her lifetime.

She would soak in a warm bath then climb into bed. In a week she would be gone to New York to meet Anna Lindfors. It was wrong for her to even believe she could make herself part of a family here. She had always been a loner. And that was what she would continue to be.

Chapter Twelve

Abel ran a hand through his hair then leaned back on the sofa. It was taking Jed a long time to return. Maybe something had happened and he ended up taking Lynne to the doctor. He rose to his feet. "Gwen, something is wrong. I need to—"

The door opened and Jed entered. Abel made tracks to meet him.

"Where's Lynne?"

Jed hung his coat on the coat rack. "Do you even care?"

A muscle twitched in his jaw. He should have expected this night to be his for getting lacerated. The knives were getting sharper with every word spoken. "Yes I care. I was upset about Samson. You know how I feel about my dog. He's all I've got left."

"Really? Seems you've been humming that tune ever since Ilene passed away. Now that a wonderful girl has settled next door to you and brought you back into the fold of your family, you push her away."

155

"Now wait a minute, Jed. I never encouraged Lynne to patch things up with my family. I insisted she not interfere. I urged us to only be friends. And I don't believe I actually pushed her away."

Jed crossed his arms. "Yeah well I'm glad it worked out this way. At least I can finally see my brother again. If she hadn't pushed the issue, you wouldn't be in my home right now."

"I didn't see you knocking down my door to get back with me after Ilene died!"

"Whoa, whoa. Hold it right there, mister. How could I when you pushed us all away? You refused to take any of our calls. Did you count how many times that Gwen even called? Did you even bother looking at your caller id? I doubt that. No not Abel. He accuses us of not caring for Ilene. Not sharing the loss that he did. And to use the lame excuse of how we didn't care for her because she had Cherokee in her . . ." Jed raked a hand through his hair. "Abel, what was that all about? I should have gone to your home and stormed that door down."

"Well, you didn't."

"And you didn't meet us halfway!"

Gwen stood between the both of them one hand palming the others chest. "This is not getting anyone anywhere."

"She's right, Abel. We were family. *Are* family."

Abel swallowed hard. "I'm sorry. I needed the support of my family and I treated each of you like outcasts. If I had to do it over, I would never have turned you away. We supported each other when our parents died. I should have—"

"Yes, you should have!"

"Jed please. I don't want the boys to hear this argument." Gwen said with soothing words. "I think everyone realizes their mistake now and is willing to make a change. I believe everyone learns from their mistakes. Don't you?"

Jed nodded. Abel did the same.

"The boys never understood any of what happened between you two. I don't want to have to try to explain this to them now. They may act mature at times but they still have little minds that don't register why things can't be the way they want them to be. They go to bed every night praying that Lynne and Abel will marry. They don't understand. I'm worried about Lynne now. If that eye sets in with bleeding, she's going to have problems. Were you able to convince her to go to the doctor?"

"No honey. She wanted to be alone. Take a bath and go to bed and forget everyone and *everything*." His eyes strayed to Abel. "Of course at the time, I didn't blame her for feeling that way. Made to feel like an outcast."

Abel inhaled a heavy breath. That had cut a hole in his heart. But he couldn't blame Jed. After all, he had spoken unkindly to Lynne at the vet's office.

"She'll go for me. I'll take her." Abel reached for his jacket.

Jed grasped his arm. "Abel, she doesn't want to see you. If you go up there and drag her out to see a doctor you'll only make matters worse. Give her some breathing time."

Abel swallowed. "I love her. I have to tell her I'm sorry."

Gwen eyed Jed. That was the first time they had

heard Abel come out and say those three words about Lynne to them.

"Yes. I realize that I love her. She has changed my life in so many ways."

This time Gwen clutched his arm. "Abel, perhaps Jed is right. You should give her some space. If you truly have love for her like you proclaim, it will grow stronger with time."

"Tell me something, brother, if you love her, are you prepared to give up one woman?"

"What are you talking about?"

"Ilene? You can't have them both. And you haven't released the hold Ilene still has on you to love Lynne the way she needs to be loved."

"You want me to just forget Ilene?"

"You never forget someone who was your first love. Someone you married and expected to live the rest of your life with. You place them in a special place Abel. Don't you understand? Lynne wasn't trying to take Ilene's place. She was trying to be herself. Love you for you. But a lifetime with Lynne won't work if she has to share you Abel."

Abel stood silent, his arms tightly clenching his sides. He breezed a kiss to Gwen's cheek. "Thank you for the coffee. For the conversation. I'll let you know about Samson."

"Please do."

"I've always had him with me but the doctor said he would keep an eye on him."

"He will," Gwen said with a loving smile.

"Jed, had Lynne been crying?" Abel had to know.

"Very much so."

"I need to see her. If she closes the door in my face

then I deserve it. But I do have to try to get her to see a doctor."

Jed and Gwen watched him leave.

"You did all you could, Jed." It was Mrs. Banter speaking. "I didn't mean to eavesdrop."

"Now, Mother, you know that isn't the truth." Gwen smiled.

"Maybe, maybe not. Why don't you and I go plan a wedding?"

"Who's getting married?" Jed asked.

Mrs. Banter fanned her apron then grinned. "Why, Lynne and Abel, silly. They just don't know the exact date yet."

Lynne was slowly running in an open field of flowers trying to reach Abel but the closer she got the further away he appeared. Why couldn't she reach him? He was so close yet so far away. And who was standing between them? She heard voices then knocking. She twisted back and forth under the covers.

"Abel, where are you? I can hear you—" The voice grew louder as she sat upright in the bed. "Abel?"

The sound was coming from her front door.

"Lynne, please come downstairs. Your chain is on the door and I can't come in."

She rubbed her hands over her face. Ouch that stung. She had forgotten the lump forming on her left eye. As she gained her footing, she realized that her body ached as if someone had been pulling her back and forth by a string. She flipped on a light and headed to the door.

"Abel, what is going on? And why are you trying to break in?" She opened the door and there he stood.

Handsome in the black jacket and lean blue jeans that fit his legs so well. She could see the tint of the dark blue shirt from the top of the unbuttoned jacket.

"Could I enter? It's really brisk outside."

Her eyes squinted. "It's late. I was sleeping."

"I didn't mean to wake you."

She remembered Samson. "Oh Abel, is it? I mean, Samson, he's not—"

"No, Doc said he needed to stay there for observance. He was even going to bunk down there to keep an eye on him. Seems he was in shock. The bleeding wasn't as bad inside as he thought it was. He was knocked semi-unconscious but he thinks he will be fine. Just a few tiny cracks that will mend easily."

"I'm glad to hear that."

"Lynne please, it is cold outside and the brisk wind is going inside."

"Abel, it's late."

"You've said that already. I refuse to go until you hear me out."

It was apparent he wasn't going to leave until she let him inside. Sighing a breath, she stood back and allowed him entrance. He shut the door behind him.

"Could we go by the fireplace? I should put another log on the fire before it burns down. I don't want you to get cold tonight." He ambled over and threw two on the fire.

"Abel, I am not an invalid. I am capable—"

"Oh Lynne." He looked into her eye. "I should have been more observant of that eye earlier. Let me take you to the clinic. It's bruising and blackening. It could have bleeding inside that needs to be checked." He extended a hand to touch her cheek but she turned her head away.

She saw the sorrow in his eyes. Why was she so quick to turn away? It had to have hurt him in the same way just like when he pushed her hand away from Samson.

He stepped back, his eyes gazing now toward the fire. "I suppose I deserved that for the way I treated you earlier. For the way I've treated you since you moved here."

She arched her brows.

"I haven't been fair to you, Lynne. Ever since you fell in my arms that day, I've felt something for you. It's been eating at me since that one day." He brushed a hand through his hair. "You got me back with my family. You made me see life again, Lynne. Look, what I said to you at the vet's office about Samson and everything. At the time I thought he was all that I had. I can't explain what I want to say. How I want to say it. Lynne, I—" He turned and linked his eyes with hers. "I'm so sorry. If there is one thing that I learned out of all this, I want you in my life with me, Lynne. Today, tomorrow, and always."

She stared at him but he couldn't make out the unreadable expression on her face. There was something different about her tonight. Even with the bruising on the left side of her eye, those big button eyes were drawing him in again. His heart was melting all over again to be nearer to her. To kiss those luscious lips of hers.

"Abel, you're a wonderful guy. One that I truly could spend the rest of my life with but I can't share you. I'm not saying you have to forget about the buried past. I would never say that. You shared a love with Ilene that no one else felt. I never was trying to take her place. I'm my own person, Abel. And I can't compete with a ghost. If we expect a love to be shared by the both of us then you have to be ready and willing to let go. And Abel, you aren't ready to bury the past and start over. I don't know if you are truly willing."

He started to reach out for her hand then pulled his hand back by his side. "But I am, Lynne. I didn't realize it until tonight." A tear misted in his eye. He allowed his eyes to search the room before resting on her again. Reaching in his pockets he pulled out her truck keys and handed them to her.

"No, keep them until you can bring Samson home. Please. I am not going to be driving much with this eye. In fact I may need someone to drive me for the next couple of days."

"Will you see a doctor in the morning? If not for me, for Gwen and Jed?"

"I'll think on it. I'm not one to go to doctors unless it is an extreme emergency. I have never liked doctors or hospitals. Guess because I never had family to be there with me."

"In this case you really do need to get that eye checked. I'm serious."

"Yes, Abel, you have expressed that already."

He shifted on his legs a bit then halfway chewed at his bottom lip. "If it means anything, Lynne, I do love you."

He wanted her in his life. He loved her. There was something about the timing that she wasn't satisfied with. She started to speak but instead chewed on her bottom lip.

"I know you love me too. Eric and Brad overheard you talking to yourself one night. They told me." He exhaled a breath. This wasn't going to be easy winning her heart back. Had he even had her heart at all? "You're right, it's late. I've kept you too long." His eyes searched her lips. He wanted to kiss her, hold her in his arms. And more than anything, he didn't want to be alone. He wanted to stay with her. Even if it meant sleeping on her sofa again. "Again I'm sorry, Lynne. So very sorry. Please make sure you lock the door. Good night Lynne."

He brushed past her sending a flow of current charging through her body. She heard the door open then closed. He was gone. Her body ached in a way far worse than any arm slinging had pronounced on her. She crossed her arms.

"Abel, oh my precious Abel." She put the chain on the door then plunged onto the sofa. She wanted to be near him forever and always too.

Abel marched into the cabin, threw the keys on the desk, then eyed the photos. Ilene was gone. She was never coming back. She would want him to find someone and be happy. To have a family. He couldn't make a life with Lynne if he couldn't bury the past.

Follow your heart.

"What?" He turned around. He could have sworn someone touched his shoulder and spoke to him. Must have been the wind howling outside. But he felt something touch him. No, his mind was too preoccupied with Samson and now with Lynne. He loved her. He wanted to pamper her and take care of her for the rest of their lives together. "Well, you blew it this time, mister. The way she cast her eyes on you tonight, I doubt she ever tells you that she loves you."

He thumbed a finger near his chin. What to do? He would have to work hard to get back in her graces. But what? First he would settle matters then do everything in his power to win her heart back. He eyed the photos once more.

"Yes, I need to follow my heart."

Chapter Thirteen

Jed opened the cabin door for Lynne and allowed her entrance. She had phoned him early asking would he drive her to the clinic. He had been more than happy to. She had been completely checked over, written out prescriptions and taken home. She was told to rest, stay out of light for the next three days. And don't touch the eye for anything. That part wasn't going to be easy. On occasion she liked to touch it to make sure there was no swelling or anything. There had been a little during the early morning but it had gone down with some ice.

Jed was placing her medicine on the counter when there was a knock at the door. He opened it and saw Abel standing there.

"I saw your car. I was curious if you persuaded Lynne to go to the doctor. I asked her to last night."

"Come in Abel, that wind is cold." He admitted Abel inside then closed the door. "Yes. She phoned me this morning, not feeling well. She is to stay out of light for three days. More or less rest. Her body took a silent beating itself. She was struggling to keep Samson from tearing Franklin Goolsby apart. And with her petite size trying to break apart a man and a big dog, you can probably imagine how she feels today."

Abel searched the room but didn't see her.

"She's changing. I suggested she get out of the car, go home and slip on her pajamas. If not then she won't stay in bed. The doc said the same thing. If people don't slip into their sleeping clothes they don't get rest."

Abel noticed Lynne descending the stairs. She had on her dark green gown and robe. She was a vision of loveliness as she descended the few stairs. The green color accentuated her hair and eyes. His heart went out to her. The blackening appeared worse for wear today.

Abel approached her. "How are you doing Lynne besides the pain?"

"I'm all right, Abel."

"I wanted to see you before I went to check on Samson. I'm glad you went to the doctor. Is there anything that I can get you? Do for you?" She shook her head. "Perhaps I should stay here with you and take care of you for the next three days."

"No. I'm capable."

"I suggested she come stay with Gwen and us but she wants to be alone."

"It's nothing personal Jed. You have a house full now. I really need to be alone. I have to get completely well before its time for me to meet Anna Lindfors.

You will still drive me to the airport when its time for me to leave?"

Sorrow covered Abel's face. She was still planning to fly to New York. And she had asked Jed to drive her to the airport. Lynne noticed the expression covering his face.

"Abel I asked Jed to drive me because I didn't know what you might have planned. And with Samson, I don't know how long it will take him to fully recuperate. The ride to Knoxville might not be comfortable on him."

"So you're still planning on going before the holidays?"

"Yes, Abel, this is important to me. I will try every possible way to return for the boys." *If you do love me, Abel, truly love me, why don't you ask me to stay for you?*

He saw the display of emotions flashing across her face. *I don't want you to go, Lynne.* "Just do what the doctor orders, Lynne. I'll go see about Samson. I'll come by with your truck."

"I told you to keep the keys until I am well enough to drive. You have to make sure Samson is well too. I've already conveyed to you that I trust you to use the truck. It's only a vehicle."

"I still could stay here on your sofa and make sure you were well taken care of until your eye heals."

"No Abel. I will be fine. Besides I wouldn't want the town to start any gossip."

"I wasn't aware they would. It wouldn't be like I've never stayed here with you before and watched after you." His tone was slightly rough. It was useless. She wasn't going to ever accept him in her life again. "If you need me Lynne, you have my number." He turned and walked past Jed. "I'll talk to you later. Give the boys a hug for me, and Gwen and the baby."

Jed rested a hand on Abel's shoulder. "I will. Let us know about Samson."

"Abel." Lynne stopped him before he stepped outside. "Would you let me know about Samson?"

"Why wouldn't I?" He walked out the door closing it sharply.

Jed looked out the window and watched as Abel took three long strides to the truck then lowered his head in a moment of silence. His brother was hurting in a worse way and there was nothing he could do. Abel had to work this obstacle out.

"Jed, I didn't mean to come across harsh. There have been so many things said. I—" She started to speak but tears wanted to mount. The doctor had said no crying.

"Lynne, you know you can't start shedding any tears. The doctor strictly prohibited any crying. You don't want any more swelling on that eye."

She inhaled a breath. "I'm not."

"Of course he didn't know you had a broken heart. I guess he figured you might shed some tears over the pain."

Lynne halfway smiled. "Tell me Jed, why does love have to hurt?"

"I don't know, hon, it just does. I've asked the same thing. You sure you can't postpone this trip until after Thanksgiving?"

"Mack has tried all that he can. You know how it is in this business?"

"Yes. Now before I leave, is there anything I can get for you?"

Abel, her eyes said. "No. You should go check on Gwen and the baby, not to mention the boys. Will you still bring them with us to the airport?"

"You bet." He kissed her cheek. "Talk to you later, sport."

Lynne watched out the window as his car drove away. She would have to do exactly as the doctor said so she would heal properly. The Monday before Thanksgiving would be here in no time and she had to make a good impression with Anna Lindfors. First impressions were always what people remembered. She had phoned Mack to make sure everything was still intact for that day. He had said it was going like clockwork. It had been good to hear his voice. Her eyes strained outside the window again. Her thoughts turning to Samson and yesterday. No, she couldn't be reminded of that day. It made her think of Abel, his words, and his sharp eyes. She decided to go recline on the sofa and flip the television channels.

An hour later Abel returned with Samson in tow. He left him lying on the front seat of the truck to go tell Lynne that the vet allowed him to come home.

"I'm sorry, Lynne. I know you were probably rest-ing. I have Samson in the truck."

Her eyes peered over him trying to see.

"He's lying down. Still a little out of it. I've got to make sure he takes it easy too. Look, if you've changed your mind, Samson and I could camp out here. I could take care of the both of you the next couple of days. It wouldn't be like when the boys were here but we could still manage to have some kind of fun if we tried hard enough." *Why don't you just tell her that you don't want to be alone in the cabin? Tell her you want to be by her.*

Her heart said yes but it was her lips that spoke. "I don't think so Abel. I do appreciate the offer, but . . . what I mean is with things the way they are, we need our own space now." She so wanted to accept his offer. But she needed more time and with each of them having their own space this would give her that time. *Abel, I have to decline your offer. I don't want to . . . oh, am I doing the right thing?*

He licked his bottom lip then crinkled his face. It would be so easy to tell her that he needed to stay. That he wanted to stay. Hadn't telling her that he loved her meant something? Wasn't it enough? "I guess a man shouldn't have to be told more than once. I've really overstepped my bounds now. I better hurry and get Samson home. I won't ask again, Lynne. You have my number." He slowly turned around and walked to the truck.

This time Lynne didn't care. She closed the door and allowed tears to swarm out of her eyes. She ambled toward the steps and marched to her bed. Maybe the pain pill she had taken just before Abel knocked at the door was settling in her system. All she wanted now was sleep. Sleep to forget the handsome man who was still making threads over her heart.

Abel looked at the number then placed it back on the desk. He cast his eyes at Ilene's photo. He lifted it and looked at it for a brief moment before placing it back on the desk. He inhaled a deep breath then

decided to make the call. He had to at least give it a
try.

Lynne had spent the last couple of weeks taking
complete care of herself. It was Monday morning and
she had packed a small suitcase the night before. Jed
had picked her up for church services. She had her
truck but he chose to pick her up. No one had seen or
heard from Abel since he had brought Samson home
from the clinic. Not even a sound from Samson stroll-
ing down to her porch. She assumed he was all right.
Now it was the Monday morning before Thanksgiving.
There had been no word from him, not even a phone
call. Of course she hadn't bothered to dial his number
either. She had tried to wash him out of her head and
heart but it wasn't even remotely being rinsed out.
Twice she wanted to confront him. Tell him it was
true. She did love him and want to be with him too.
But now it was her stupid pride that forbade it.

She glanced in the mirror at the jeans and yellow
pullover sweater she was wearing. It would be warm
enough with her leather coat. When she got into New
York she would have time to change before she met
with Mrs. Lindfors. Mack said it would be around
eight before they all got together at the office. She had
something unexpected to come up and had to slightly
change her plans. It was all right with Lynne. It only
pushed her flight earlier returning. She really didn't
want to disappoint the boys. And she wanted to see
Abel sitting across from her at the dinner table. She
had missed him so much the past couple of weeks.
With the change of events, thanks to Mrs. Lindfors
having to change her routine for the holidays, it made

it possible to keep her promise to the boys to return by turkey day.

The sound of a knock interrupted her thoughts.

"Hi, Aunt Lynne," Eric said. "Are you ready? Brad and Daddy are in the car. Now you will be back for turkey day?"

She eyed his little face so full of spirits. Why couldn't adults always have that simplicity as little children when they got older? She sent him a warm smile.

"I'm ready. Let me get my bag." She heaved the small bag in her arm, locked the door and headed to the car.

"Have you seen Uncle Abel?" Brad asked when she got in and closed the door. "We haven't seen him or Samson."

"No hon, not for a while now."

"Daddy hasn't either. He must be out hunting for a turkey or something. You will be back for turkey day, right Aunt Lynne?"

"Yes dear. Eric asked me the same thing."

"But you didn't answer me," Eric proclaimed.

She turned to Jed who had only nodded when she got in the car. The boys had been doing all the chattering. "Can we make one quick stop to Gene's before we head out? I need to drop off some more designs that he is having someone make for me."

"No problem. Gwen said to tell you to have a safe trip and be calm."

"Thanks, Jed. I am trying my best."

The boys and Jed were looking at some new shipment of items that had come in Gene's store while Lynne handed him the paperwork.

"Think this will be a problem?"

Gene eyed the drawings. "No. My man can do that with ease." He placed the drawings under the table for safekeeping. "Saw Abel in here with a woman the other day."

Lynne's eyes perked up. So did Jed's.

"Another woman?" It caught in her throat.

"Yes. Some nice-looking sophisticated woman. He was showing her one of the items he had carved."

"So she was like a client or something?"

"Oh, she was something all right. Had her hand wrapped right inside his arm. Some looker she was." He cleared his throat. "Not meaning you aren't, little lady. This woman was just different."

So Abel had another woman. It sure didn't take him any time to forget about her. She shot her eyes to Jed remembering the first time he told her to stay away from Abel. Well he had been right about the man breaking her heart. Well, he was free to have whomsoever he wanted. And to think he declared his love for her.

Eric and Brad stood by her side holding some figurines up that were on display.

"Oh wow, look at these, Aunt Lynne," Brad said.

"Just came in yesterday and some tourist has already gathered up a handful," Gene remarked.

Lynne was still frozen in time with Abel and the woman. Brad continued to hold the figurine up toward her face.

"Look, it's you Aunt Lynne and Uncle Abel. I'm sure it is."

She came back to earth and glanced at the figurine in Brad's hand. It indeed was a replica that favored her and Abel. She looked at the others on the counter. There was one of her and Samson. One of her and the boys. Another of her holding a tiny infant. Then one of her, Abel, and Samson. They might not have been the true identity but they sure were replicas of them.

"Uncle Abel sure made a lot of them," Eric stated.

Her eyes clocked with Gene's then Jed's.

"What did you say Eric?"

"Uncle Abel. He made a lot of them this time. All the figurines of people and animals in this store, Uncle Abel makes for Mr. Gene."

This time? She recalled the ones she saw in his cabin that day. She had mentioned his were better than the ones in the shop. She looked at them again. "You said Abel just brought them in recently?"

"Yes, I—" Gene stopped. The cat was out of the bag now. She would know the boy was telling the truth.

"Why didn't you tell me that day, Gene, that Abel made these?"

"Abel doesn't like others to know what craft he possesses. You can ask Jed."

"It's true, Lynne. Abel is quiet when it comes to that. He makes them and brings them down to sell."

She swept her eyes over them once more. "Jed take me home."

"But what about your flight?"

"I've changed my mind. Please I need to go home." She slapped some bills on the counter. "Gene this should cover what I'm taking with me."

Jed wasted no time in getting them all settled in the car then headed back to the cabin. He was glad that she wasn't going. The boys chanted so much about it

that Jed finally told them if they didn't quiet down;
Aunt Lynne would change her mind. They immediately put a stop to their chattering but smiled under
their breath.

Jed stopped the car and Lynne got her bag out.

"Thanks Jed," she said, sitting the bag on the
ground.

"What are you going to do?"

"I'm not sure. I want to know who this woman is.
I want to know why Abel didn't tell me about the
designs he was working on."

"Uncle Abel and Samson." Eric was the first to
jump out of the car and go running to the dog. Brad
followed.

Lynne turned around to see an undeniably attractive
man coming her way. With each stride he stepped toward her, her heart fluttered. She left the car door open
and stepped halfway to greet him. Jed turned off the
motor and waited for the boys.

"Abel." She stopped inches short of him.

"Lynne."

Her heart soared at the simple way he let her name
roll off his tongue. Too many days had passed since
she had seen or heard from him.

"You aren't going to New York?"

"I had a change in plans. I will need to call Mack."

"What happened?"

"I stopped at Gene's on the way to drop off some
designs."

He knitted his brows together.

"Why didn't you tell me, Abel? The day I saw the
figurines. Then I saw the ones in your cabin. I mentioned you could do a better job than the ones the man

did in Gene's store. I saw the ones you did today. Of me, of us, and Samson." Her eyes reflected to Samson. He was back to himself again. She was glad. "I could tell that those had been done out of love, Abel. You did one of us, Abel," this time a tear fell from her eye down to her cheek.

Abel reached to stop it. His finger alone sent chills down her spine. Oh how she had missed his touch. She slightly closed her eyes and opened them. The palm of his hand touched her cheek.

"Your eye still has some light staining but it does look better. I wished that I could have been there for you to help make it all better. I've missed you Lynne."

"I've been so foolish, Abel."

"No, we never say fool or foolish." He smiled and her heart did a double spin.

"The boys were right. I said I loved you. I meant it. I do love you Abel. I love you so much it hurts. I was wrong to deny my love for you. To continue to ignore my heart. To close that door when you came over and apologized to me for your words . . . when you told me you loved me. I was . . ."

"Hurt? I don't ever want you to feel that hurt again. They do say you always hurt the one you love. I guess we both have filled the bag on that one. Funny how the eye can't see what the other feels inside his heart."

Surprise cropped her face.

"Franklin Goolsby. He got my number. Phoned me and told me why he was here. How Samson was so protective of you that day. Samson knew already that you belonged to me. I should have listened to my dog. Franklin even offered to pay for Samson's dog treatments. I told him no. We were fine. You were too. He sends his best for us."

He eased down on one knee and took hold of her right hand. "Lynne, there is something that I want to ask of you. Something that I hope you will say yes to." His other hand reached in his jacket pocket and pulled out a ring. "I took it out of the case so it would be easier for me to place on your finger. I didn't want to let go of your hand once it was inside mine again."

He inhaled a breath.

"Lynne Marie Murphy." He noticed her eyes widened. "Spoke to Mack. He told me your middle name. Now can we get serious here?" A light smile creamed her face. "Lynne Marie Murphy, will you please consent to being my wife for the rest of our life together? I mean someone has to look after you. You fall from ladders. You trip over rocks when you're running. And you don't know how to duck your head when someone is swinging a right fist your way."

Jed stood out of the car and watched. He couldn't believe his eyes. Eric, Brad, and Samson stood silent. They too couldn't believe it. Samson perched his head sideways.

A wide smile enveloped her lips. "Yeah, I suppose that you are correct about all that. I would be most honored to be your wife, Abel Mason. Most honored."

He stood up and pulled her into his arms, his lips gently brushing hers in a warm kiss.

Hands clapped, cheers of joy resounded and then a woman's voice spoke.

"I was wondering when you were going to say yes, dear. If I wasn't already married, I would have snatched this young man up three days ago."

Lynne stood and eyed the woman who had spoken. "Anna Lindfors?"

"In the flesh," she said, gliding over to congratulate the both of them. "This young man has done nothing but talk about you since I arrived. I have never seen or heard a man so much in love with one woman in my life."

"But . . . I don't understand. I was supposed to meet you."

"True. But your young man phoned me after you had your little falling out. He was so afraid that he would lose you. One thing he didn't want was to say good-bye to another loved one. Told me how he needed me to come down here. He was afraid that you wouldn't be back in time to share the holiday with him. Promised to show me the sights of Gatlinburg and surrounding areas. Even promised me a swing and bench to put out on my farmhouse in New York."

Lynne eyed Abel. He had phoned Anna. He cared enough for her to try to work it out between them. For a moment their eyes only lingered to each other as if they both knew what the other was thinking. Yes, he really did love her.

"I don't know what to say, Mrs. Lindfors."

"Absolutely nothing. After I saw the drawing of Abel and his dog, I knew you were the one I wanted to commission to do all my illustrations."

"What about your publicist?"

"If she doesn't approve, guess I'll have to hire a new one." She laughed.

"So you're the sophisticated lady that Abel was escorting in town? Gene mentioned that Abel had brought a real looker in his store."

She laughed again. "I like that man." She glanced at her watch. "Well, Abel, we have to hurry to meet that appointment. Of course we didn't expect her back here so soon, did we?"

"No. We thought you would get to the airport and see your flight had been changed. Then Jed would bring you back. He knew nothing about this."

"Sure didn't," Jed announced.

"No, only those two lovely ladies, Gwen and Mrs. Banter," Anna remarked. "My husband is down with Mr. Banter now. Guess they are discussing golf. Well, here comes the limo now. You and Abel will ride in it. I will ride with Jed and the boys."

"Ride where? I don't understand."

"Why, to discuss your wedding, dear."

Surprise layered Lynne's face.

"We have been so busy working on plans. Actually Mrs. Banter and Gwen have been the ones working on this project for almost a week. Abel even showed me a gown he would like to see you in. Oh yes, Mr. Banter wants to walk you down the aisle. They found the most precious wedding chapel."

"This is too fast."

"Oh dear, we didn't mean it to be. Your young man so wants to be with you. He wanted some spontaneity. I guess we got carried away with the ambience of everything that we were hoping that you would accept his proposal and jump at the chance to marry him before the holidays."

"Yes, I can tell." She smiled.

"Lynne, I never meant to move so fast," Abel mentioned. "I took matters into my own hands without giving any thoughts of how you would feel about any of this. It's true. I wanted you to be my wife when we share Thanksgiving together. I don't want to live another night without you in my arms, Lynne. I love you. And look at the boys, do you want to disappoint them?"

Eric and Brad put on their best smiling faces.

She released a hearty laugh. "Not on your life." Her arms cupped around Abel's neck as she pulled his lips down to hers. This time her kiss exploded shivers all over his body.

Abel pulled away and looked into her button eyes. "Wow, and I thought the day you fell in my arms was an explosion. Look, we can go discuss the wedding with the others and just tell them we want to wait. Give it some time. Maybe after the holidays."

Lynne playfully slapped his chest. "Not on your life, mister. If those dear women have gone to that much trouble for me, I want to be spontaneous. I love that." She clapped her hands together. "The more I think about it, this is really romantic, Abel. I will never forget this day."

"I wanted to make it a day that you would remember always."

She leaned upward and kissed his cheek. "You truly have. I love you so much, Abel."

"I love you too."

"Okay, here's the limo. I'll go with Jed. Come on boys. Bring Samson."

Anna was chattering worse than the boys. Lynne didn't know who was more excited about the events, her or Anna.

"Yes, Mrs. Lindfer," Eric said.

Jed started to correct when Anna raised her hand. "Honey, just call me Miss Anna."

"Okay, Miss Anna. You know Brad and I prayed every night for this to happen."

"And your prayers have been answered."

Lynne swung inside the limo then Abel. He folded her into his arms and held her closely to him.

"Oh Abel, this is the best day of my life."

"It is mine too, sweetheart. I love you more than you will ever know, Lynne."

"Oh I think I know, Abel. I feel the same for you." She pulled the figurine from her purse. "I made sure to purchase this one Abel. I had to have the one that Brad handed me."

He breezed a kiss to her cheek. "I have the first one I made in the cabin. I just have to bring it to you."

"Then we will have two to sit side by side."

"Yes we will." She buried her head in the hollow of his shoulder. It felt good to be this close to him again. And soon she would be Mrs. Abel Mason. "Wow, how could a girl get so lucky in one day? A husband, a dog, a family, and a contract with Anna Lindfors in one day."

Abel tightened his arms around her. "How could a man get so lucky to have an angel fall in his arms?"

"I am actually going to plan my wedding with a family. This means so much to me, Abel."

"I can tell in your voice and on your face, sweetheart." He leaned over and wet her lips with a soft kiss.

Lynne lost herself in the kiss and in the feel of his arms. A feeling of security and deepened love. The same she felt the first day she plummeted into his strong arms.

The last of the ornaments had been placed on the tree when Brad pulled the one out with Ilene's name on it. He looked at Abel.

"Uncle Abel, what do we do with the ornament with Aunt Ilene's name?"

Abel cast a look Lynne's way.

"Where did you normally hang it, Brad?" Lynne smiled.

"Right over near Uncle Abel's where yours is hanging."

"Then why not hang it on the other side? You know her ornament should always be put on the tree every year too." She cast her eyes toward Abel.

"Yes Brad, I think that is a good place," Abel said as he circled his arm around Lynne's waist.

Brad hung the ornament on the tree then stepped back as Jed plugged in the lights.

"Wow," Eric said.

Lynne kissed Abel. "I love you, darling."

"I love you, sweetheart."

"Mom, Dad, can Samson sleep in our room tonight, please?" Eric asked.

"I suppose. Now tell everyone good night and go to bed," Jed answered.

After the boys and Samson had disappeared to their room, Gwen cuddled Ilene in her arms. "I know the two of you wanted to be alone in your own cabin. But the boys insisted you be here for an early Christmas."

"Abel and I will have other nights to share in our

cabin." Lynne rested her head on his arm. "I wouldn't have missed this one here."

"As long as the two of you are going to be comfortable down here."

"With Lynne near my side, I will always be comfortable."

"Then Jed and I will turn in. Santa will be arriving early, won't he dear?"

Jed was busy checking the gifts under the tree. "Oh yes. And your mother will have us up earlier than Santa."

Lynne and Abel snuggled under the blanket as they lay near the fireplace. A smile crossed her lips as she watched the flames dance.

"What's that smile for, darling?"

"I'm so happy. I have the contract with Anna. Plus there are days that I will be sketching downtown. You are opening your cabin as a craft shop. Mrs. Banter is going in business with Mabel designing cakes and other bakery items. I'm so glad they decided to move down here. It's like I have a real mom and dad now, too. It's a dream come true for all of us. A family and a business all in one."

Abel hugged her closer to him.

"I have a loving husband and the best dog in the world. I'm so happy, Abel. I never imagined anyone could be this happy. I never want this feeling to disappear."

"I'll make sure that it never does." He breezed a kiss over her lips. "Lynne, how I love you."

Lynne watched the twinkling of the lights on the tree. Abel liked the way her eyes twinkled along with the lights and the dancing fire flames.

"What do you want Santa to bring you for Christmas when he arrives?"

"Oh Abel, Santa gave me my gift when I fell into your arms. He gave me my ready, willing, and Abel person to share the rest of my life with. You're all I ever need from Santa."

"I feel the same, Lynne. Thanks to you, I have my family back. And the sweetest woman alive." He laced his hand inside hers. "We better go to sleep or Santa won't arrive at all. Then the boys will be disappointed."

"I don't want the boys ever disappointed. We owe them a great deal."

"I'd say we sure do."

While the fire began to die down and lights from the tree sparkled back and forth, Lynne rested her head in the crook of Abel's shoulders. Two little boys and a dog looked down from the top of the stairs and smiled. It was the best gift ever.